TANK & FIZZ

THE CASE OF THE MISSING MAGE

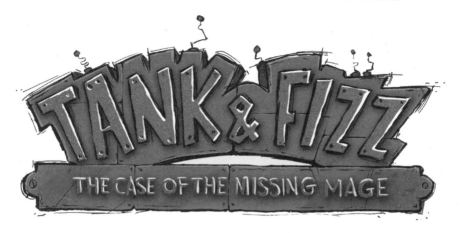

TANK & FIZZ
THE CASE OF THE MISSING MAGE

BY

LIAM O'DONNELL

ILLUSTRATED BY

MIKE DEAS

ORCA BOOK PUBLISHERS

Library and Archives Canada Cataloguing in Publication

O'Donnell, Liam, 1970–, author
Tank & Fizz : the case of the missing mage / by Liam O'Donnell;
illustrated by Mike Deas.

Issued in print and electronic formats.
ISBN 978-1-4598-1258-1 (paperback).—ISBN 978-1-4598-1259-8 (pdf).—
ISBN 978-1-4598-1260-4 (epub)

I. Deas, Mike, 1982–, illustrator II. Title. III. Title: Tank and Fizz.
IV. Title: Case of the missing mage.
PS8579.D646T345 2017   jc813'.6   C2016-904578-1
                              C2016-904579-X

First published in the United States, 2017
Library of Congress Control Number: 2016950094

Summary: In this illustrated middle-grade novel and third book in the Tank and Fizz series, a goblin
detective and technology-tinkering troll must mix magic and gadgetry to defeat the evil doom mages.

*Orca Book Publishers is dedicated to preserving the environment and
has printed this book on Forest Stewardship Council® certified paper.*

Orca Book Publishers gratefully acknowledges the support for its publishing programs provided
by the following agencies: the Government of Canada through the Canada Book Fund
and the Canada Council for the Arts, and the Province of British Columbia through the
BC Arts Council and the Book Publishing Tax Credit.

Design by Jenn Playford
Illustrations and cover image by Mike Deas

ORCA BOOK PUBLISHERS
www.orcabook.com

Printed and bound in Canada.

20 19 18 17 • 4 3 2 1

For Ail, an amazing sister and true friend.
—Liam O'Donnell

For Faye — Mike Deas

CHAPTER ONE
A Case that Sparkles

The frigid waters of Fang Harbor churned below me. Screams filled the air.

"Reel me in, Tank!"

The screams were mine.

I was a tail's width above Fang Harbor's icy waves, hanging by my belt.

It was the second day of Fungi Break. A week off school. No classes, no books, no homework. This goblin was very happy about that. Yeah, I said goblin.

The name is Marlow. Fizz Marlow. I'm in the fourth grade, and I solve mysteries. I'm also a goblin. You know, green scales, big ears and a tail that my mom says is "cute." You okay with green monsters

1

and cute tails? Good. Because there's a whole bunch of monsters in my hometown of Slick City, under Rockfall Mountain. Monsters like my best friend and detective partner, Tank. She's a troll. No tail but lots of gadgets. Trolls like to tinker with technology, and Tank is no exception. Her tinkering can save the day or land us both in big trouble.

And right now, I was about to land in something very cold and wet.

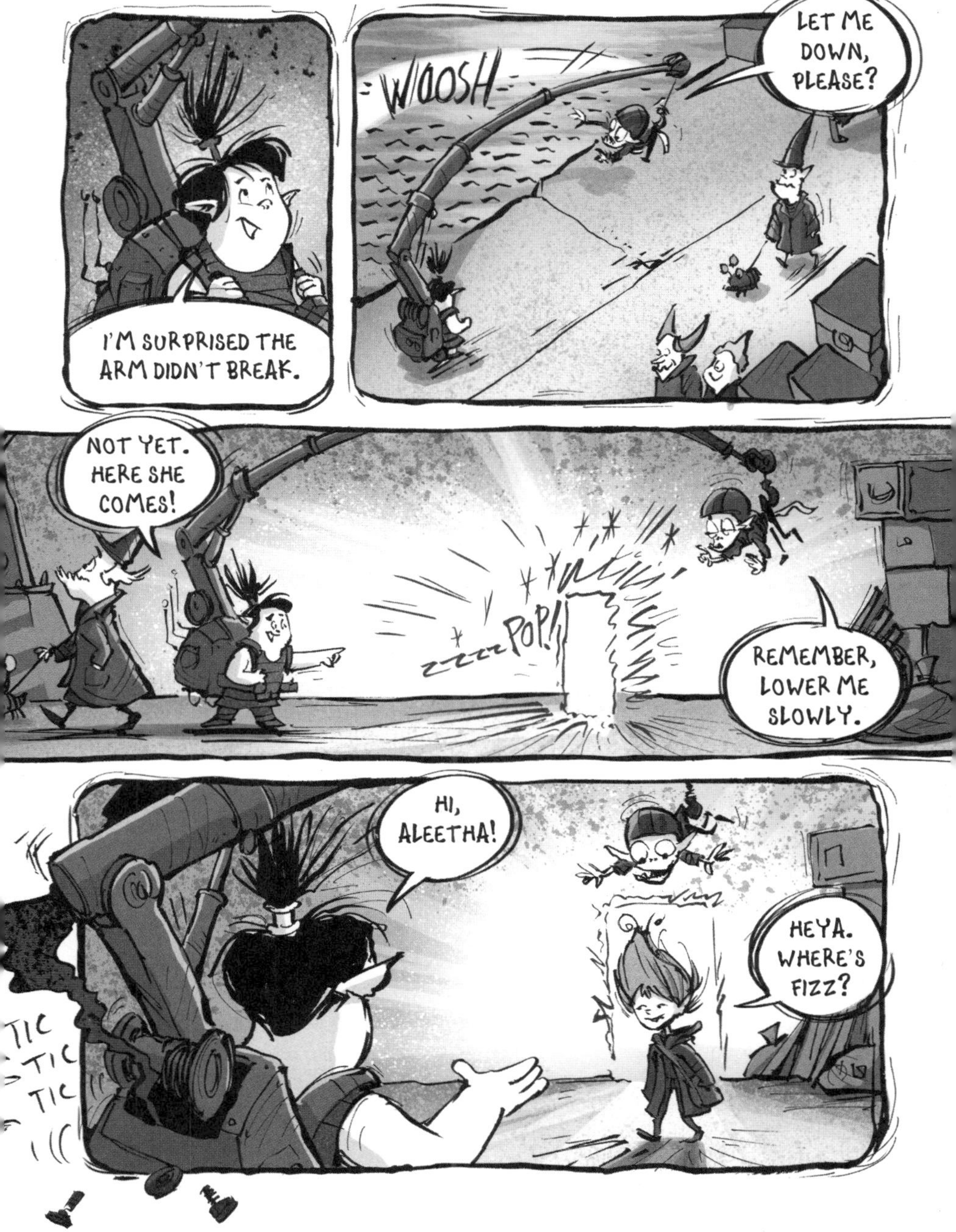
I'M SURPRISED THE ARM DIDN'T BREAK.
WOOSH
LET ME DOWN, PLEASE?
NOT YET. HERE SHE COMES!
zzzzPOP!
REMEMBER, LOWER ME SLOWLY.
HI, ALEETHA!
HEYA. WHERE'S FIZZ?
TIC TIC TIC

Aleetha helped me to my feet. "Quit fooling around."

I was too sore to yell at Tank. And she probably would have been too busy putting out the fire in her backpack to hear me anyway.

Aleetha helped me out of the harness. She was a wizard, but she unbuckled the straps with the speed of an engineer. Well, okay, she was a wizard-in-training. She had gone to our school until she left to learn magic at the Shadow Tower. Now she liked to surprise us with her tricks, as well as help us solve mysteries. The look on her face told me something was very wrong.

Aleetha unsnapped the last buckle and flopped onto a rock. She looked sadder than a goblin on the last day of summer vacation. That goblin being me.

Tank took the helmet from me and turned to Aleetha.

"What's wrong?"

"My teacher is missing!" Aleetha sounded like she was going to cry.

"So what's the problem?" I said. "If Mr. Mantle disappeared, I'd throw a party."

"Fizz!" Tank said. "Old Tentacle-Face isn't so bad."

"Then why have I got a stack of math homework taller than me at home?"

"Maybe if you actually did the homework, it wouldn't be a giant stack," Aleetha said.

"An interesting concept. I'll take it under consideration."

"Seriously though," Tank said. "Why are you worried about your teacher? She's a grown wizard who can take care of herself."

"True," Aleetha said. "She went to the lava pits of Gornash to gather data for her research project on the fire lizards that live there. It's hatching season, and she is counting their population."

"Sounds like fun," I said.

"I know!" Aleetha said, totally missing my sarcasm. I made a mental note to work on that. "She was supposed to be back yesterday, but she hasn't returned."

"I'm still waiting for the part where this becomes something to worry about," I said.

Aleetha turned to me. "I know this is hard for you to grasp, Fizz, but some monsters actually like school. For them it is fun."

"I'm not even going to try to grasp that."

"The little guy does have a point, Aleetha," Tank said. "Your teacher is a bit late returning from a research trip. What's the big deal?"

"The big deal is the Wizards' Summit," Aleetha said. "It starts today. Wizards from all over Rockfall Mountain have come to the Shadow Tower. Professor Lasalan is supposed to be there."

"Maybe she's just late," I said. "She's still counting baby lizards or something."

Aleetha shook her head slowly. "I don't think so. Something isn't right. Yesterday I got this in the mail."

She pulled a small metal cylinder from her wizard's robes. I ducked behind a rock. Mages like Aleetha can do strange stuff with the things they pull from their robes. Like turn goblins into rock slugs.

"It's all right, Fizz," Aleetha said with a chuckle. "It's not a spell."

I stepped out from behind the rock. "Then what is it?"

"I don't know. It arrived yesterday with my name on it. It's from Professor Lasalan."

The cylinder was about as long as Aleetha's hand, the color of muddy water and round at each end. The surface was completely smooth, with no markings or writing.

"Maybe it was a gift," I said. "Some sort of magic present."

"I don't know what it is," Aleetha said. "I've cast every spell I know to identify it, and I keep coming up with nothing."

"That's because it's not magic." Tank took the cylinder from Aleetha and looked at it closely. She smiled at both of us. "This is an example of high-quality troll engineering."

Aleetha got to her feet and stepped back. "It's technology?"

"Nothing but the finest," Tank said. "It's a Holographic Express Message Tube, or HEMT for short."

"Message tube?" I said.

"It seems your teacher has a soft spot for trollish tech." Tank wiggled her ears at Aleetha.

"A wizard use technology? Never!" Aleetha scowled.

"Okay, let's not start another magic-versus-technology war," I said. "Tank, what does your amazing HEMT do?"

"Stand back and I'll show you." Tank put the tube on the ground. "You just have to press the button on the end."

"Button?" Aleetha said. "I didn't see a button."

"That's because you're not a troll." Tank's ears wiggled again.

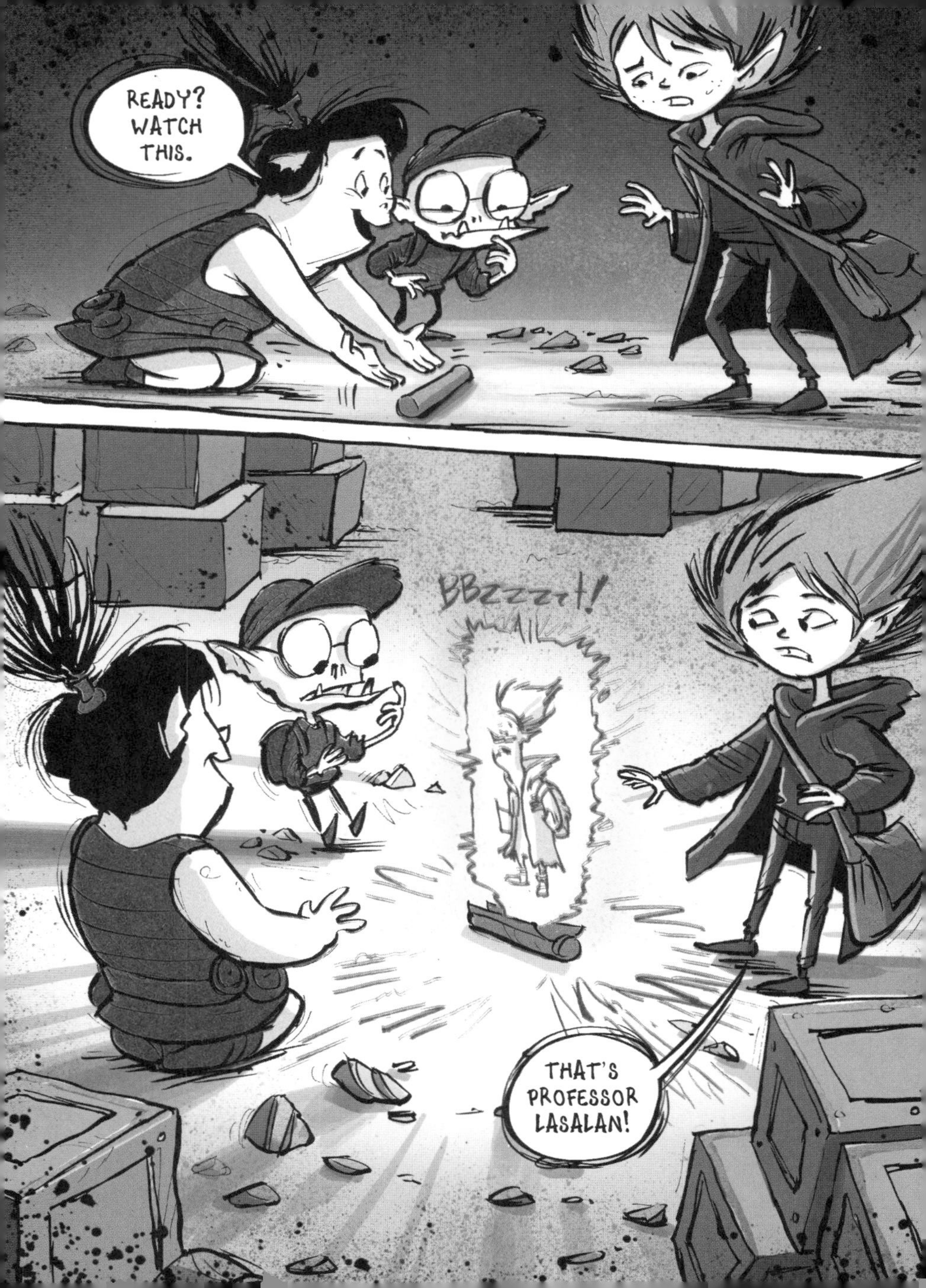
READY? WATCH THIS.
BBzzzzt!
THAT'S PROFESSOR LASALAN!

"I knew she was in trouble!" Aleetha said.

"What are the black cloaks? And why are they returning?" I asked.

"I have no idea." Aleetha stared at the tube with her eyes narrowed. "Play the message again, Tank."

Black smoke began to stream up from the HEMT.

"That might be a problem." Tank stepped away from the tube.

In seconds it was enveloped in a thick, dark cloud.

"It's on fire!" Aleetha shrieked. "Stop it!"

"You're the lava elf. Fire is your thing." I coughed. Smoke billowed into the air around us.

Then the smoke stopped as quickly as it had begun. Tank stepped closer to the tube and waved away the remaining tendrils of dark smoke. The HEMT was now just a charred hunk of metal.

"It must have been programmed to self-destruct," Tank said. "Your mentor didn't want anyone else to hear her message."

Aleetha didn't take her eyes off the charred HEMT. "We need to talk to Mr. Lorof."

"And where is he?" I asked.

"He runs a bookshop in the Mage District." Aleetha tightened her robe. "If we hurry, we'll catch him before he closes for the day."

"Mage District?" I gulped. Suddenly I wished I was back dangling over Fang Harbor.

CHAPTER TWO
Skull Surprise

The streets smelled of magic.

But that's what you get in the Mage District. You also get narrow streets lined with bookshops, potion vendors and wand-repair shops. The Mage District is the go-to place for spell ingredients, potion supplies and anything else that scares the scales off a goblin like me.

"Why does the air smell like a crowbar?" Tank asked.

"That is the scent of magic." Aleetha breathed deep and stood watching the crowd of monsters mill around us. "Isn't it wonderful?"

"It's wonderful if you like sniffing nails." Tank

looked up from the screen on the gadget in her hands long enough to scowl at Aleetha. "At least with technology you get to hold the metal and not just smell it."

"Tank, we're guests here in the Mage District," I said. "Can we please be polite to all the magic types around here? I'd like to reach fifth grade without being turned into a slugnat."

Tank looked around. "I'd like to know why this place is so crowded."

"You weren't kidding," said Tank.

"What is a wizards' summit?" I asked.

Aleetha's eyes lit up. "The Wizards' Summit is a gathering of all the wisest wizards from Rockfall Mountain and beyond. They're all meeting in the Shadow Tower this week to talk wizardy stuff."

"Sounds terrifying," Tank said.

"Depends on your views on magic."

Aleetha hurried through the crowded street without another word. Tank gave me a worried look, and we fell into step behind her.

Monsters and magic don't really get along. Unless you're an elf like Aleetha. Elves can use magic and live to tell the tale. When goblins, trolls or ogres try to get their magic on, they usually end up as piles of dust, turned into rockgrubbers or banished to the planes of never-ending homework. Technology is a different story. Monsters love their tech like a snapfish loves to snap. From gadgets to gizmos, technology rules in Slick City—except in the Mage District.

We took a sharp turn down a narrow alley and emerged in a wide plaza with a fountain in its center. The fountain sparkled with the telltale sign of magic, but it wasn't what caught my eye.

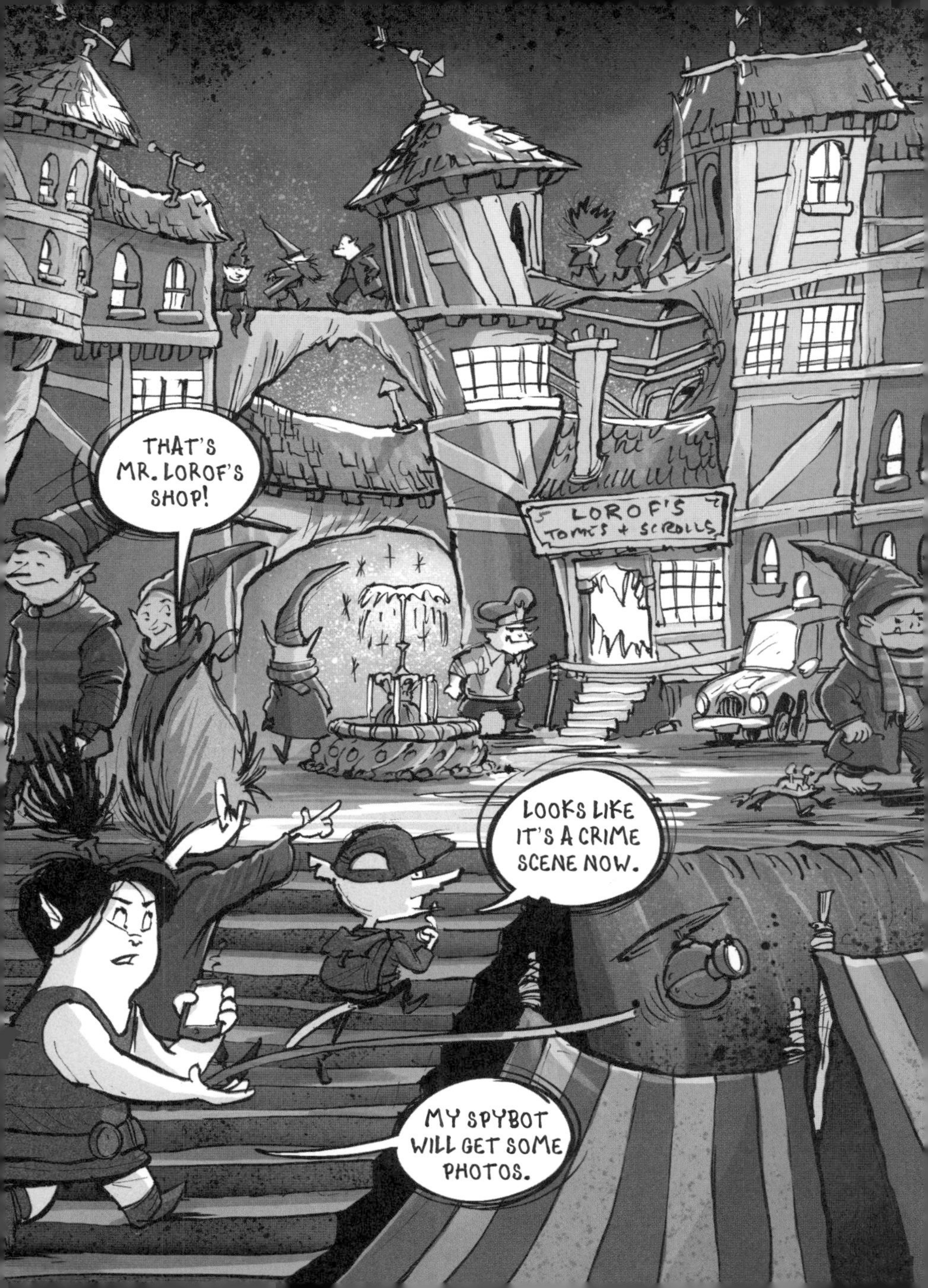
THAT'S MR. LOROF'S SHOP!
LOROF'S TOMES + SCROLLS
LOOKS LIKE IT'S A CRIME SCENE NOW.
MY SPYBOT WILL GET SOME PHOTOS.

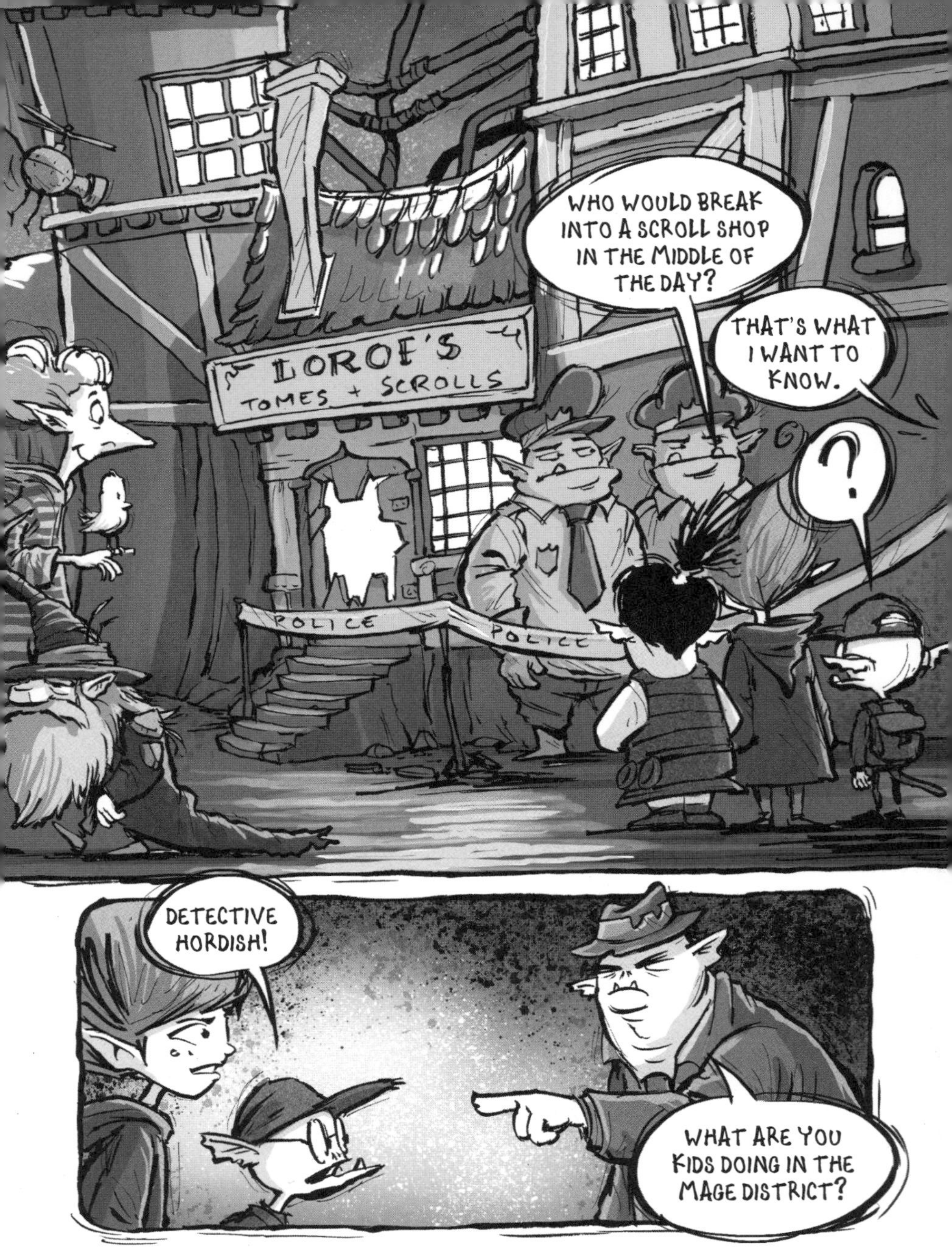
LOROF'S
TOMES + SCROLLS
POLICE
POLICE
WHO WOULD BREAK INTO A SCROLL SHOP IN THE MIDDLE OF THE DAY?
THAT'S WHAT I WANT TO KNOW.
?
DETECTIVE HORDISH!
WHAT ARE YOU KIDS DOING IN THE MAGE DISTRICT?

"We came to meet our friend, Mr. Lorof," Aleetha said.

Detective Hordish glared at her like he was figuring out if she was telling the truth. Or maybe he was figuring out what to have for dinner. You can never tell with that old ogre. Hordish is okay as far as adults go. He doesn't like us snooping around his investigations, though, especially when we solve them before he does.

"Mr. Lorof is not here," he said eventually.

"Do you know where he might be?" I asked. "Or why the door to his shop is smashed in?"

"I'd like to know why you're not in school," Hordish said.

"It's the Fungi Break! We're off school for the whole week."

"That so?" Hordish grunted. "Well, go find another crime scene to play in. This one is mine."

A cloud of purple smoke appeared from nowhere near the middle of the plaza. The cloud churned and grew larger. A slender elf stepped from the cloud and stood beside the fountain.

Aleetha ducked behind Tank at the sight of the new arrival.

"Inquisitor Quantz," she squealed. "Hide me!"

The clouds wisped away to nothing as Inquisitor Quantz marched straight for the crime scene. He carried a tall staff carved from a material I didn't recognize. His robes were covered in intricate designs that changed color with each step. Just watching the mage's robe made my stomach churn, like the time Tank's mom took us around the harbor in her tugboat.

"Detective Hordish!" The inquisitor pulled back his hood to reveal a face sharp enough to cut rocks. "What is the meaning of this? What are you doing here?"

Hordish turned to meet the mage and sighed. "I'm investigating a robbery, Quantz."

"You will do no such thing!" Quantz pulled himself to his full height and towered over the ogre. "This is Shadow Tower territory. The shadow guards will deal with this matter. Go back to your own neighborhood. I'm sure there's a goblin stealing baked goods somewhere."

"We've been over this, Quantz." Detective Hordish unslouched himself and tried to meet the elf eye to eye. He managed eye to chest, but that's what you get with those annoyingly tall elves. "Your troop of weirdos can investigate crimes that happen inside the

18

Shadow Tower. The real police will take care of everything outside the tower. And that includes the Mage District. Unless you want Mayor Grimlock breathing down your neck, I suggest you return to your books and let us do our job."

Quantz's purple eyes flared at the detective's words. I'm not sure if wizards have figured out how to shoot lasers from their eyes, but I bet old Quantz wished he could.

"Very well," he snapped. "But I want a full report of your findings."

"You will get it, as always." Hordish didn't take his eyes off Quantz. For a slow-witted ogre, he was doing a good job of keeping the wizard in his place.

Inquisitor Quantz's head turned sharply in our direction. My tail curled, and I wanted to hide behind Tank too. But there was no room.

"Aleetha Cinderwisp!" Inquisitor Quantz said like he was smashing boulders.

Aleetha stepped out from behind Tank. She tugged at her robes and stared at her feet as if they were suddenly the most fascinating things in the whole mountain.

"What are you doing here?" Quantz continued, happy to find a new victim to bully. "You are needed in the Shadow Tower. You should be welcoming your summit buddy and joining in the festivities."

"Yes, sir," Aleetha mumbled with only a glance up at Quantz. "I was just looking for Mr. Lorof. He is missing, and so is Professor Lasalan!"

Quantz snorted at the mention of Aleetha's mentor. "That old fool? Never mind her. She is probably too busy dancing with fire lizards and has forgotten about the Wizards' Summit. She will show up eventually, as she always does."

"You don't understand!" Aleetha started, but a wave of Quantz's slender hand silenced her.

"It is you who doesn't understand, my dear." The elf moved his hand in a slow circle. Wisps of purple smoke appeared at Aleetha's feet. "Return to the tower like a good lava elf."

The purple smoke grew around Aleetha's feet and rose until it was drifting around her shoulders.

"I've got to go, guys," she said as the cloud engulfed her head.

When the smoke vanished, Aleetha and Inquisitor Quantz were gone.

"And we thought Principal Weaver was strict," Tank muttered.

Detective Hordish walked back to the crime scene. He stopped in front of the yellow tape, like he had just remembered we were there.

"You two should scram, unless you want to be picked up for interfering with an investigation."

"We were just leaving!" Tank said.

"No we weren't!" I said.

"Yes we were." Tank grabbed my arm and pulled me to the far side of the plaza.

I shook her off and sat on the edge of the fountain.

"We can't leave yet," I said. "We don't know who broke into Mr. Lorof's shop or even why they did it. And we have no idea where he's gone."

Tank looked around nervously.

"That's probably a good thing," she said. "Fizz, this is the Mage District. That means magic, remember? I want to help Aleetha, but I don't want to go sticking my nose in wizard business. We should just leave while you still have all your scales."

I pointed toward a dark alley. "Or we could follow them."

Two elves stood across the plaza, watching Mr. Lorof's shop. Their faces were hidden under the deep hoods of their robes. They huddled in the shadows and watched Hordish and his officers continue their investigation.

"Who cares about them, Fizz?" Tank said. "They're just curious tourists or something."

"The magic is dulling your detective skills," I snapped. "Look at what your tourists are wearing."

Tank's ears stood straight out.

"Black robes!" she said, loud enough for Mayor Grimlock to hear in his mansion.

The elves heard it too. They looked across the plaza and straight at us. Without a word, they turned and ran down the alley.

"Sorry," Tank muttered.

"Apologize later," I hissed as I ran after them. "Let's see where they're going."

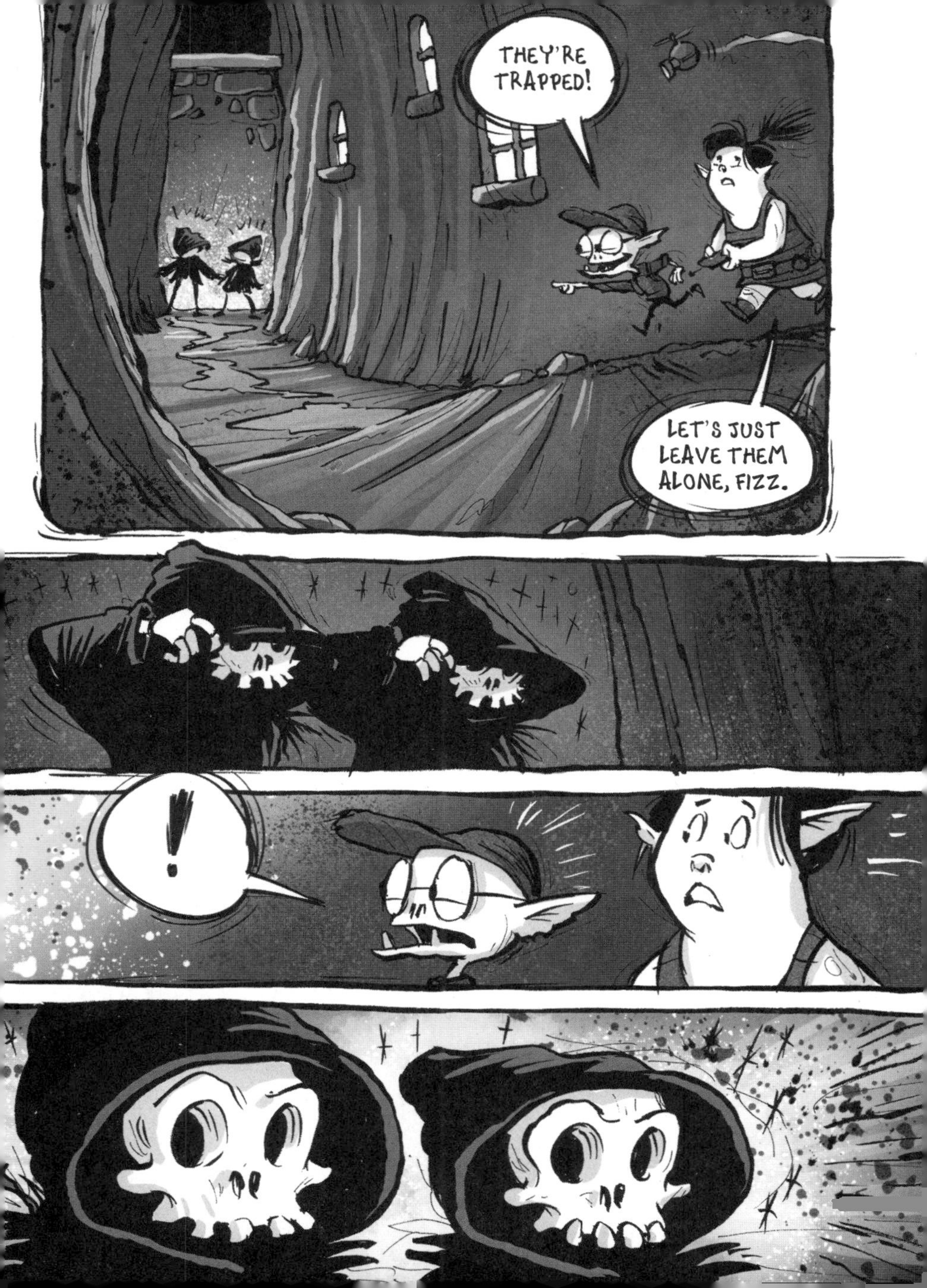
THEY'RE TRAPPED!
LET'S JUST LEAVE THEM ALONE, FIZZ.
!

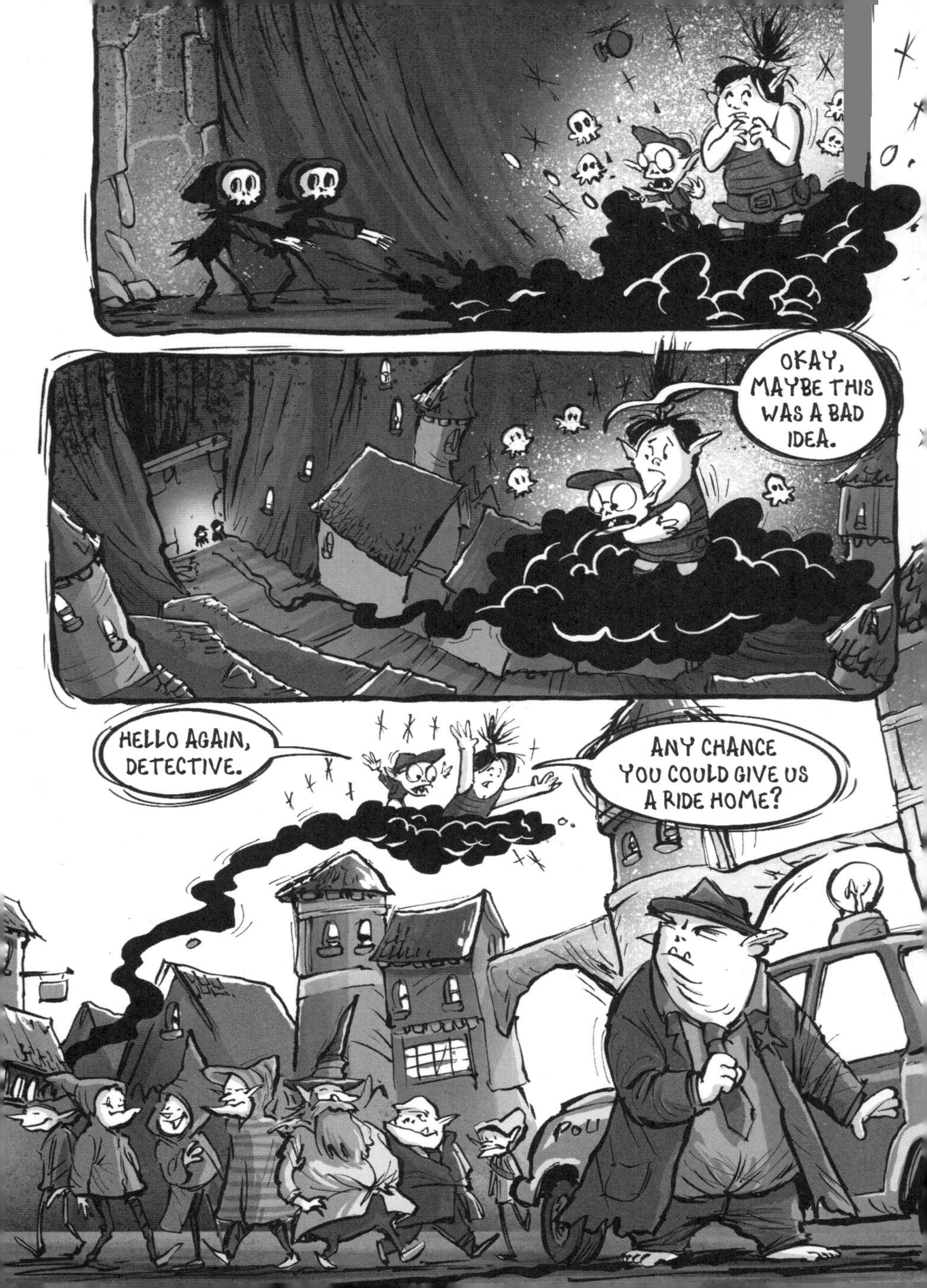
OKAY, MAYBE THIS WAS A BAD IDEA.
HELLO AGAIN, DETECTIVE.
ANY CHANCE YOU COULD GIVE US A RIDE HOME?
POLI

CHAPTER THREE
Talking Tugs with Trolls

Skulls haunted my dreams all night.

They were still swirling around my brain as I walked to Tank's cave the next morning. And with those cackling bone-heads came a lot of questions. Who were those elves in the black robes with the skulls for faces? What had happened to Mr. Lorof and Professor Lasalan? Why were Tank and I getting mixed up in a magic mystery?

My phone buzzed in my pocket. Tank's grinning face appeared on the screen when I answered the call.

"Pick up the pace, Fizz," she said. "You've been moving slower than a cleaning slime since you left your place."

"I always walk slowly when I'm thinking," I said. "How do you know where I am anyway?"

"Simple!" Tank's grin doubled in size on my phone's screen. "I configured my phone to search for your phone's signal and then matched it with the digital map of Slick City. As long as you have that phone in your pocket, I can track every step you take. Isn't that cool?"

"It's terrifying," I said. "I don't want to be tracked."

"Then get rid of your phone."

"But I need my phone!" I said. "Everyone has a phone. I don't want to be the only one without one."

"Then you're going be tracked." Tank shrugged. "And you're going to be late if you don't pick up the pace. I have something to show you."

I shoved the phone back in my pocket and turned down Tank's street.

Her cave is easy to spot. It's the one with the half-built boat in the driveway. Tank's mom is a tugboat captain in Fang Harbor, but she also fixes up old boats in her spare time. I don't know anything about boats, but I know a troll needs to tinker, and Tank's mom is no different.

As I arrived, Mrs. Wrenchlin stepped out from behind a small fishing boat missing half its hull.

"Morning, Fizz." She wiped her hand on a slick-covered rag and peered at me over her round-rimmed glasses. "I heard you had an adventure in the Mage District yesterday."

"We were helping Aleetha," I said.

Mrs. Wrenchlin shook her head slowly. "Be careful with magic, Mr. Detective. It's not like technology. You never know what it's capable of."

"That's exactly what my mom said." I kicked at a pebble at my feet.

"Your mom is a very smart goblin." Mrs. Wrenchlin sighed. "I hope you listen to her better than Tank listens to me."

My phone buzzed again. Tank's muffled voice came from my pocket.

"Quit yapping with my mom and get down here, Fizz!"

"I didn't even answer it!" I said. "How does she do that?"

"That's my daughter, the technology genius." Mrs. Wrenchlin beamed with pride. "You'll have to ask her. She's in her workshop."

Tank's workshop was packed with tools and technology. Neatly labeled bins filled with wires, circuits and other tech pieces sat on shelves that ran along the walls. Tank was parked at her workstation. Above the table, a screen hung on the wall. One look at the screen and I thought last night's dreams had returned to haunt me.

No surprise there. What else would you expect in the Mage District? But if those elves were hiding their identities with a magic spell, they were probably hiding something else. Did they know where Mr. Lorof and Professor Lasalan had disappeared to?

"Those two didn't just wander by the plaza yesterday," Tank said. "They were there for a reason."

"To break into the scroll shop," I said.

"But the only thing they took was Mr. Lorof," Tank said. "The spybot snuck in through the door when Hordish's officers weren't looking. This is what they saw."

Tank brought another set of photos onto the screen. They showed the inside of the scroll shop. The door lay on the ground, blasted off its hinges by something, but everything else was in place. Leather-bound books lined the shelves. Scrolls sat in their holders, neatly rolled and stacked. At the back of the shop, the cash register sat untouched on the counter.

"So it wasn't a robbery," I said.

Tank shrugged. "In a way it was. They just weren't stealing money. They were stealing the bookshop owner."

"We need to talk to Aleetha."

Just then Tank's phone buzzed.

"Speak of the wizard!" Tank tapped her phone, and Aleetha's face filled the big screen above us.

GET OVER HERE. I FOUND MR. LOROF!

CHAPTER FOUR
Under the Cloak

The bus dropped us off in front of the Shadow Tower.

Elves of all shapes and sizes hurried along the wide road that led through the massive gates at the base of the spire. Just seeing the colossal wall of dark stone that ran around the tower set my scales on edge. Behind those walls, the Shadow Tower reached all the way to the rock ceiling high above Slick City.

Carved from a single piece of obsidian, the Shadow Tower had appeared from nowhere long ago when Slick City was just a collection of huts. It was a gift from the Mages of the Spire, the council of wizards that dwelled deep under Rockfall Mountain. At first, the Shadow Tower was home to a few wizards who advised the small but growing number of citizens of Slick City. Each year, as more monsters arrived in Slick City, more wizards appeared in the tower. Now the city was one of the biggest in Rockfall Mountain, and the Shadow Tower was one of the best magic schools around. Elves from all across the mountain and beyond came to study magic inside the dark walls of the Shadow Tower. Today, it seemed like every elf with a touch of magic in their bones was here. And it felt like they were all staring at Tank and me.

Tank tugged at the tool belt around her waist as she scanned the busy scene.

"I've never seen this place so crowded."

"They must all be here for this wizards' party," I said.

"It's not a party," said a familiar voice behind us. "It's a wizards' summit, which is twice as much fun as a party."

I spun around to see Aleetha sitting on an ornately carved bench with a large backpack at her feet.

"How did you get here?"

She chuckled. "Relax, Fizz. No magic this time. I've been sitting here since you arrived. You two were just busy acting like wide-eyed tourists and didn't see me."

"Can you blame us?" I stepped out of the way of an elf with her head buried in a map. "All these wizards are making me a little jumpy."

"You want to see jumpy?" Tank held up her phone and showed Aleetha the photos of the two skull-faced wizards we had chased down the alley. "These two made Fizz jump higher than a hungry mudspringer."

"You were scared too!" I growled.

Aleetha took the phone and studied the photo.

"You're right," she said after a minute. "Those two are hiding their faces with some spell. And they're wearing black cloaks. I've never seen wizards in black cloaks."

"Professor Lasalan said something about black cloaks."

Aleetha nodded. "She said they were returning."

"Returning from where?" Tank said. "And why?"

"Whatever it is, it can't be good." A shiver ran down my scales at the memory of being carried through the Mage District on their cloud of skulls.

"The strange thing is that none of the magic domains have black cloaks," Aleetha said.

"Magic domains?" I asked.

"There are different types of magic, Fizz," Aleetha said. "Each type of magic is called a magic domain."

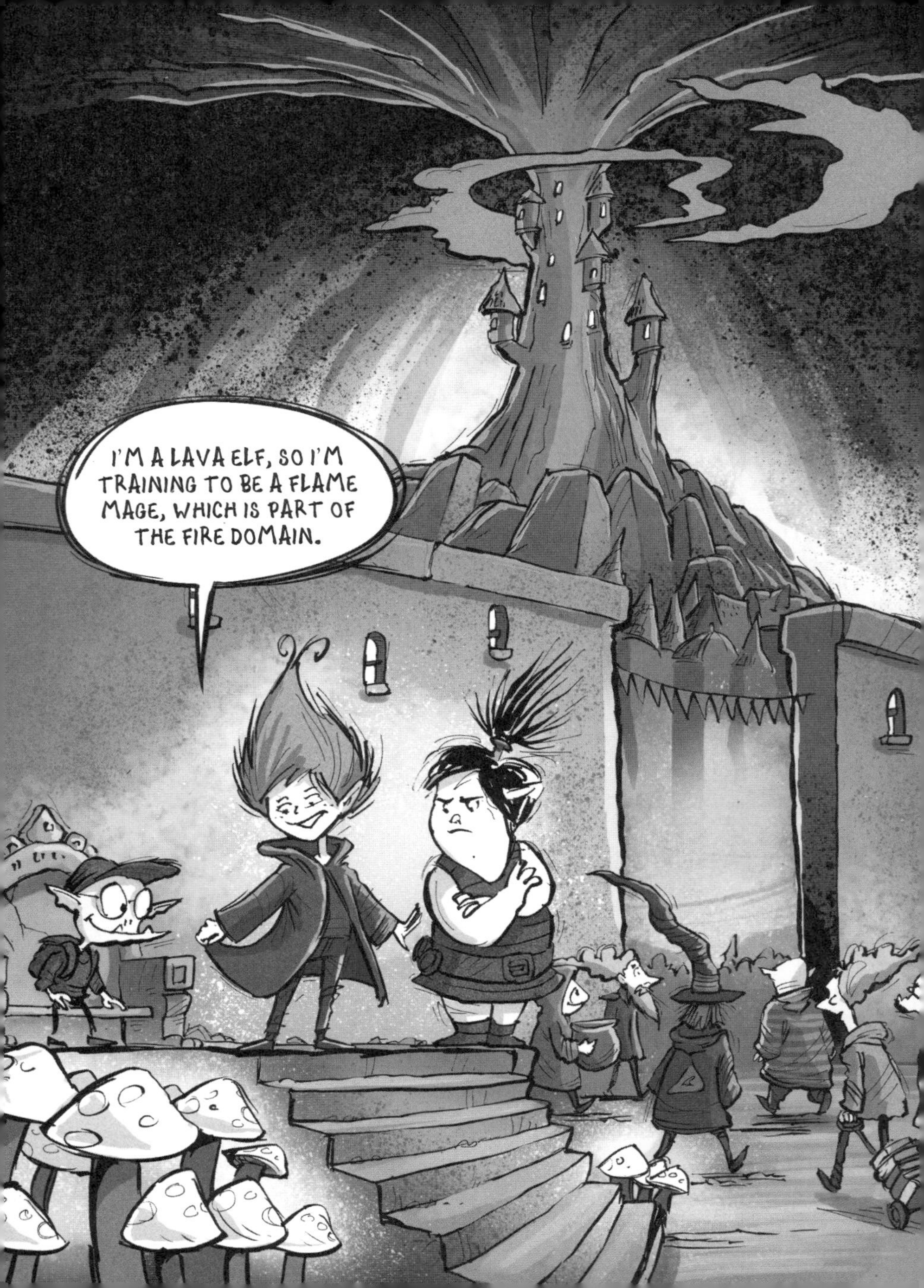
I'M A LAVA ELF, SO I'M TRAINING TO BE A FLAME MAGE, WHICH IS PART OF THE FIRE DOMAIN.

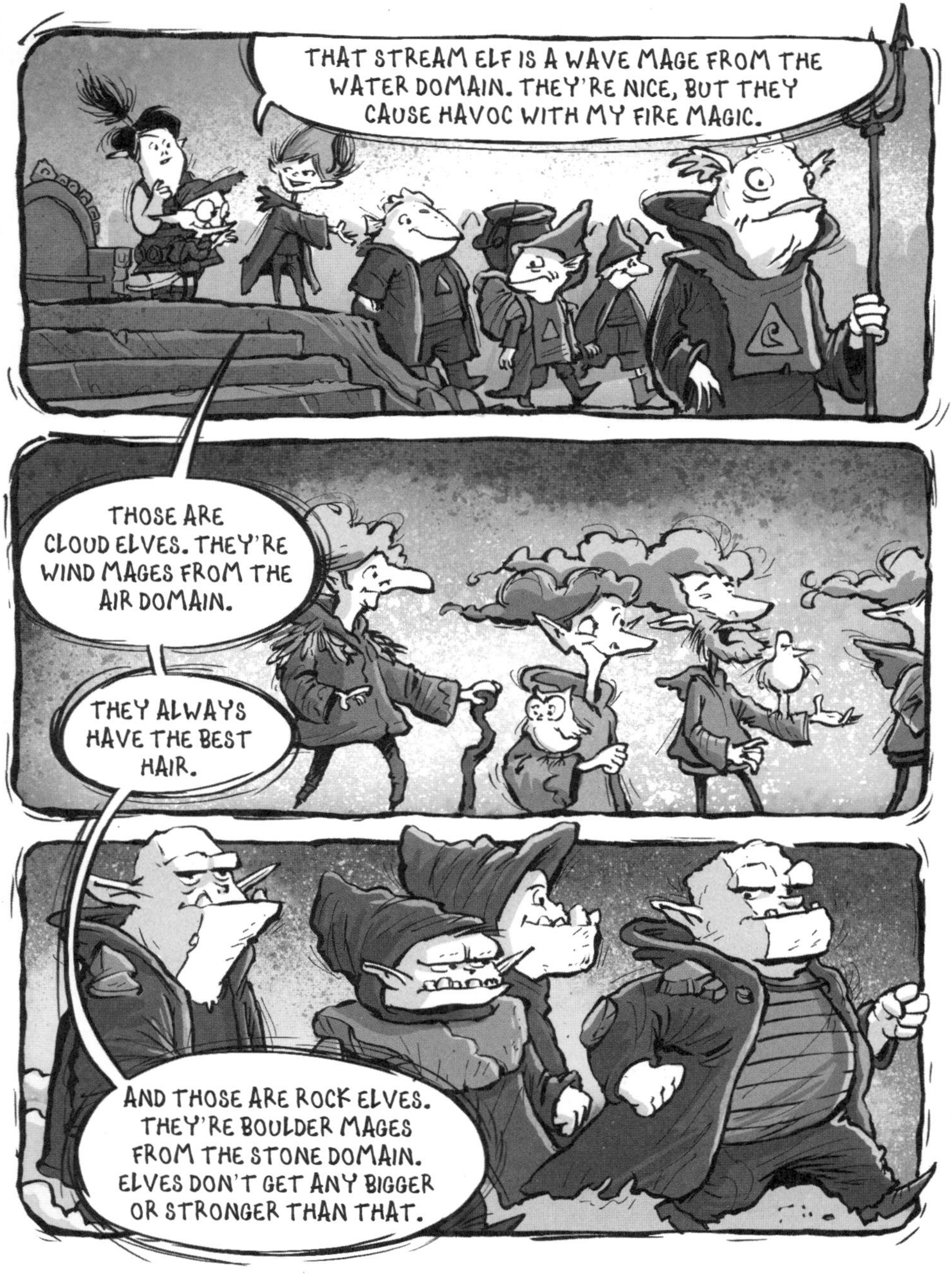
THAT STREAM ELF IS A WAVE MAGE FROM THE WATER DOMAIN. THEY'RE NICE, BUT THEY CAUSE HAVOC WITH MY FIRE MAGIC.
THOSE ARE CLOUD ELVES. THEY'RE WIND MAGES FROM THE AIR DOMAIN.
THEY ALWAYS HAVE THE BEST HAIR.
AND THOSE ARE ROCK ELVES. THEY'RE BOULDER MAGES FROM THE STONE DOMAIN. ELVES DON'T GET ANY BIGGER OR STRONGER THAN THAT.

"There are plant mages, too. If you're lucky you might see one." Aleetha spun to face us. "But, you won't see any wizards in black cloaks."

"Just on the wizards who attacked us," I said. "I don't get it."

"Neither do I," Aleetha said. "We can ask Mr. Lorof about it when we see him inside."

"Inside?" Tank's ears stiffened. "Inside where?"

My stomach felt heavy, like I'd eaten rocks for breakfast. "Please don't say the Shadow Tower."

"The Shadow Tower." Aleetha grinned.

Tank gripped her tool belt like it might jump off and run away, which is exactly what I wanted to do.

"No way I'm going in there," she said. "I can feel my technology going haywire already."

"We're here to talk to Mr. Lorof," I said. "Not to get turned into grubnugs by an angry wizard."

Aleetha sighed. "Do you think I'd let you get turned into grubnugs?"

Tank looked at me, ears quivering with uncertainty.

"The answer is no," Aleetha snapped when we didn't answer. Her fiery lava-elf eyes blazed into us. "I agree that magic can be dangerous, but so can technology!"

Tank opened her mouth to speak but shut it quickly

under Aleetha's glare. "Whether it's stolen slimes or runaway robots, you know that both magic and technology can cause chaos when in the hands of the wrong monster. I fear that's happening again. Professor Lasalan is in trouble and needs my help. And I need your help. But we can't do this if you don't trust me."

"We trust you." Tank relaxed her grip on her tool belt. "It's kind of scary being this close to stuff I don't understand."

"Now you know how elves feel about all troll technology," Aleetha said.

"What?" Tank looked up, eyes wide. "You don't like technology because you're scared of it?"

"Of course we are!" Aleetha said. "You said it yourself. It's scary being close to stuff you don't understand."

"Like me and math!" I said.

Tank's glare melted the grin from my face.

"You just don't listen in class," she growled. "If you stopped using math class as your nap time, you would understand it."

"You have a point," I said. "How about we call a truce? Tank and I will try not to be so scared of magic, and Aleetha will trust in technology a little more."

"I can work with that," Aleetha said.

Tank nodded. "Me too."

"Excellent." Aleetha reached into her backpack. "Now put these on, and let's go."

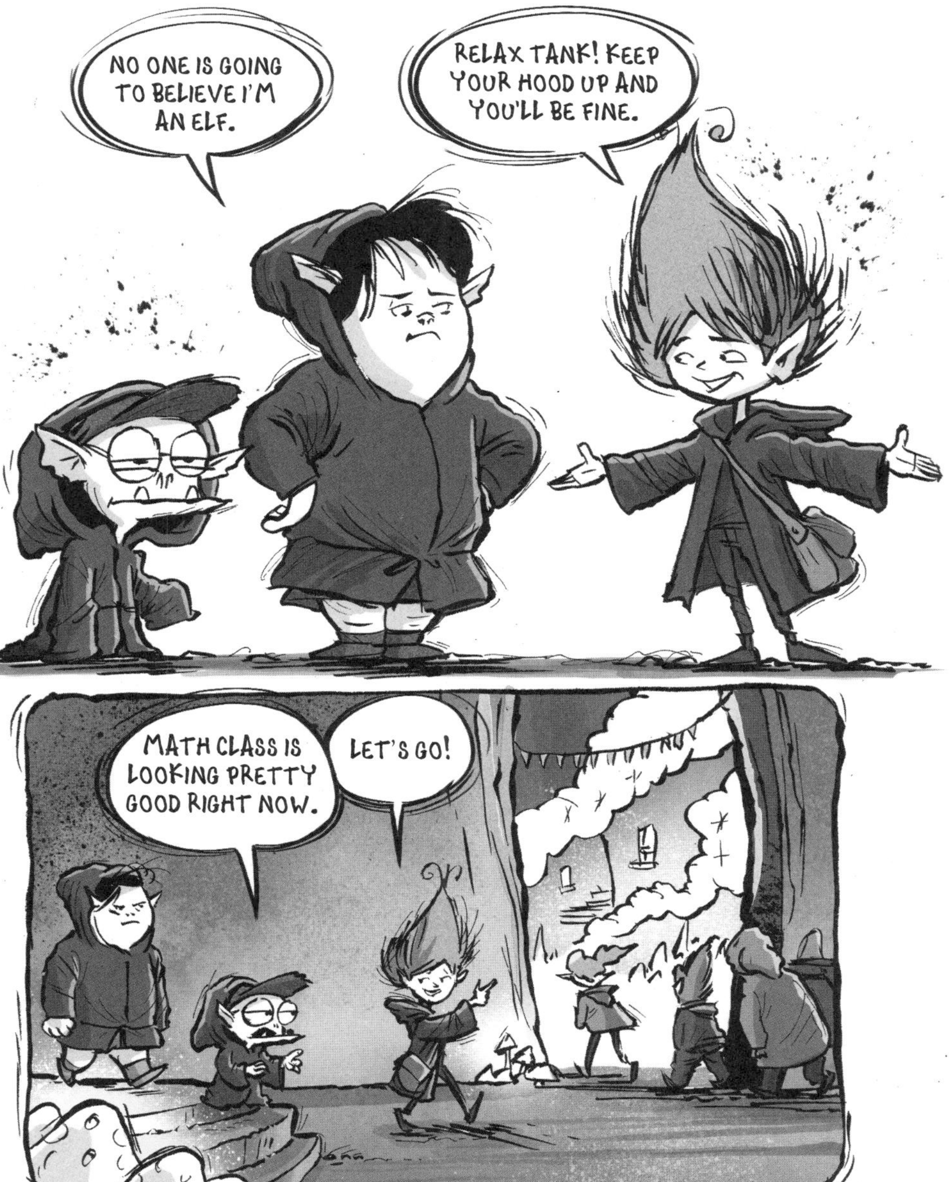
NO ONE IS GOING TO BELIEVE I'M AN ELF.
RELAX TANK! KEEP YOUR HOOD UP AND YOU'LL BE FINE.
MATH CLASS IS LOOKING PRETTY GOOD RIGHT NOW.
LET'S GO!

CHAPTER FIVE
Into the Tower

I had never been so happy to be ignored.

My heart pounded louder than one of Tank's machines. No one looked twice when Tank and I followed Aleetha into the line of wizards at the main gates. Who knew how long our luck would last? All it would take was one sharp-eyed elf to spot my tail or Tank's trollish feet, and we were grubnug stew for sure.

"This thing itches." Tank tugged at the neck of her cloak. "Why don't we use one of your shape-changing potions?"

"I'm barely more than a novice myself, Tank," Aleetha whispered. "My spells won't fool the wizards inside the tower. Once we get to Mr. Lorof, you can take off the cloaks."

"You mean if we get to Mr. Lorof," I muttered.

My neck itched too, but it wasn't because of the wizard's cloak. I was walking right into the heart of magic with only a hood to hide me. I trusted Aleetha. It was the other spell-slingers I was worried about.

"Just keep moving," Aleetha said. "The shadow guards are busy today with these crowds. They won't care about a bunch of novice wizards like us."

Aleetha's words did little to quiet my thudding heart as we passed through the gates.

My glasses nearly fell off my snout at the sight beyond the wall. My whole life I had wondered what lay on the other side of the dark brick wall that surrounded the Shadow Tower.

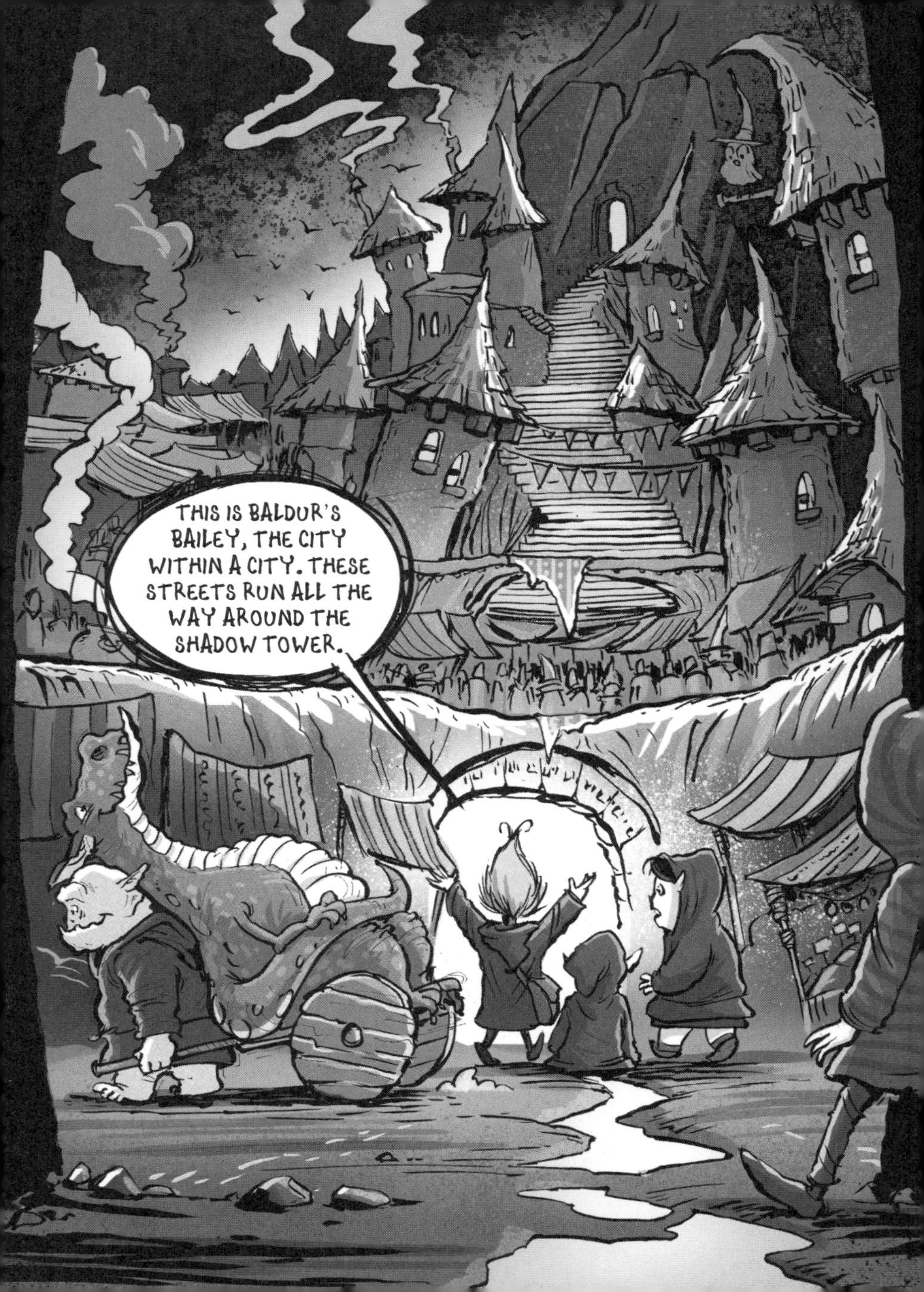
THIS IS BALDUR'S BAILEY, THE CITY WITHIN A CITY. THESE STREETS RUN ALL THE WAY AROUND THE SHADOW TOWER.

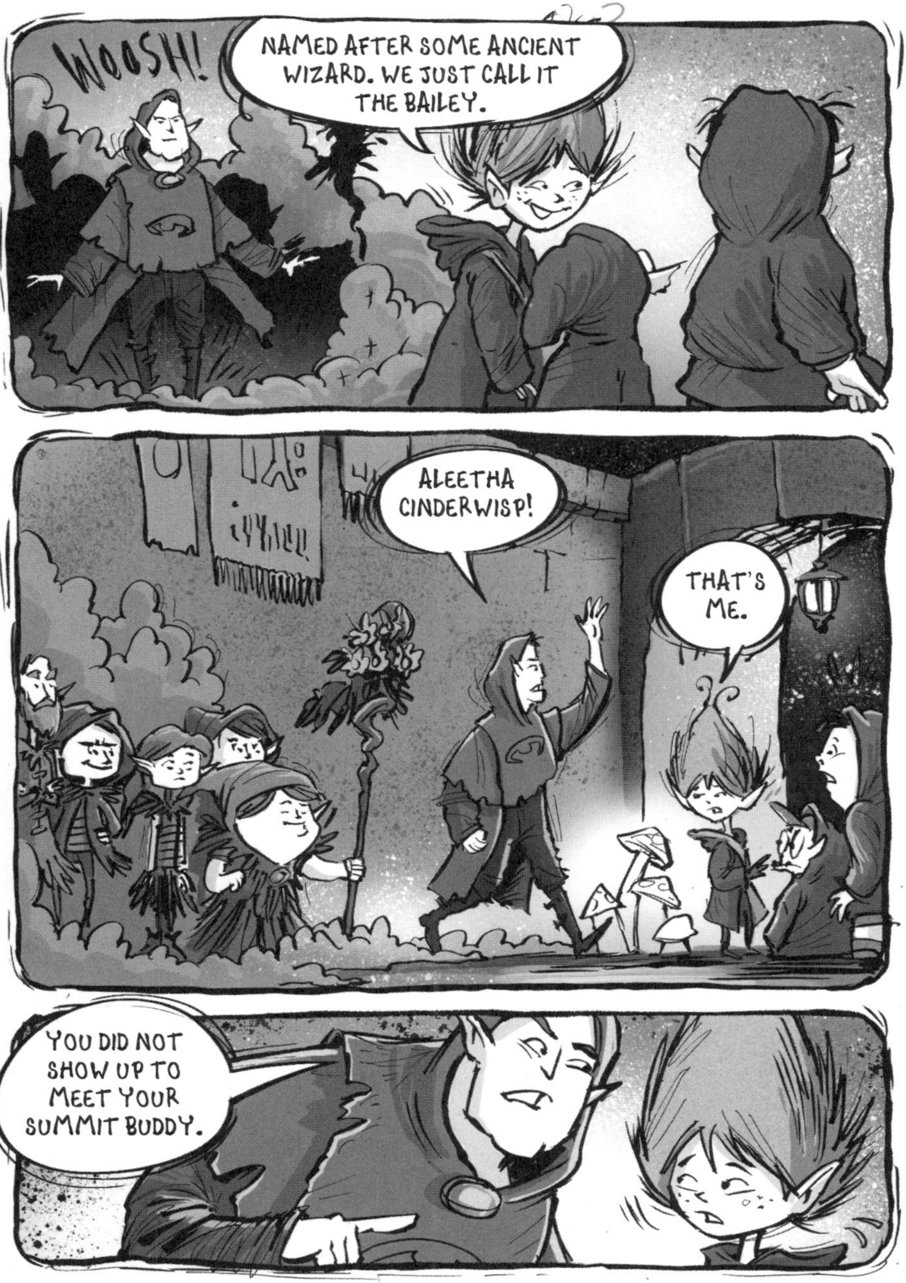
WOOSH!
NAMED AFTER SOME ANCIENT WIZARD. WE JUST CALL IT THE BAILEY.
ALEETHA CINDERWISP!
THAT'S ME.
YOU DID NOT SHOW UP TO MEET YOUR SUMMIT BUDDY.

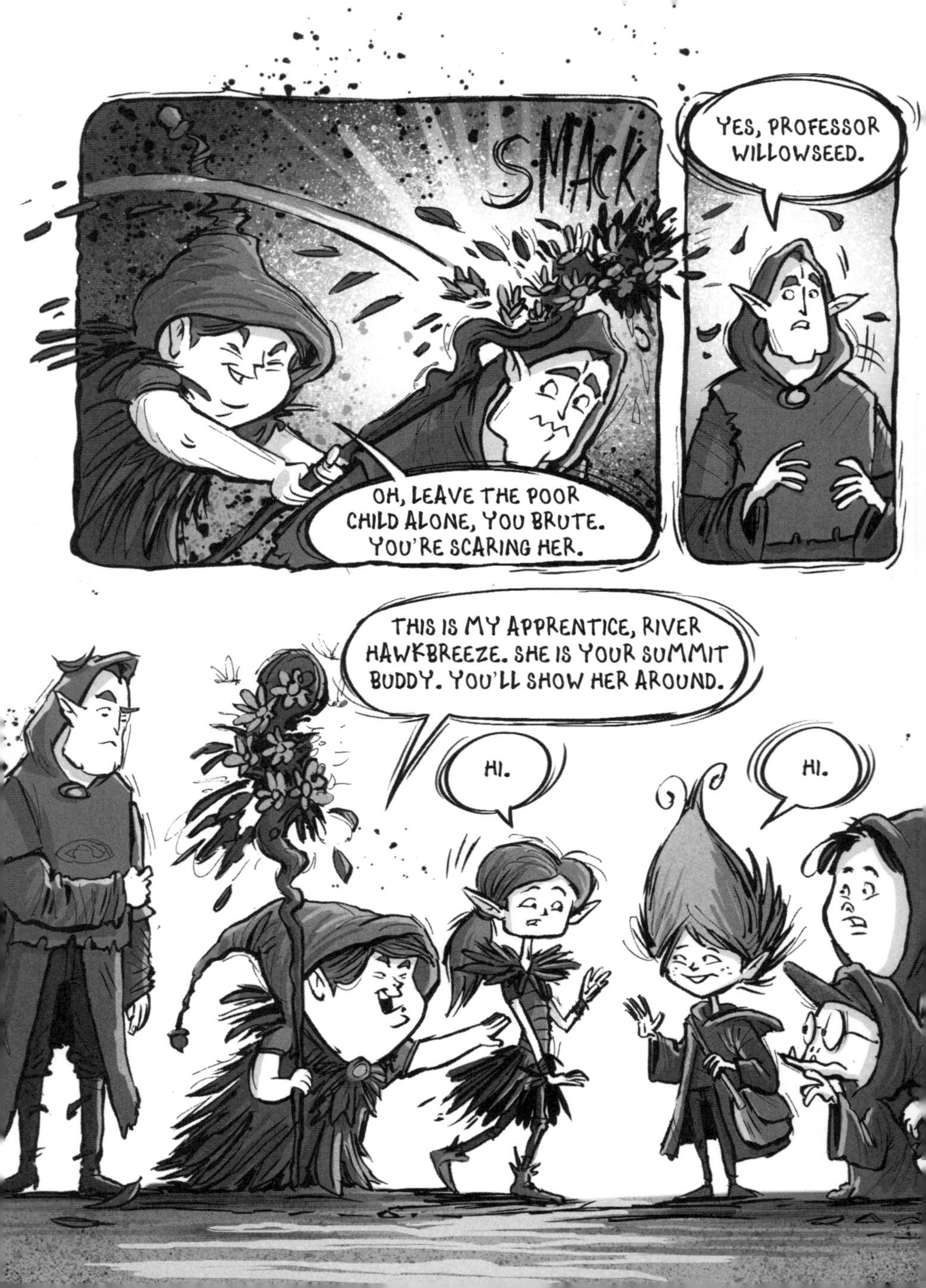
SMACK
OH, LEAVE THE POOR CHILD ALONE, YOU BRUTE. YOU'RE SCARING HER.
YES, PROFESSOR WILLOWSEED.
THIS IS MY APPRENTICE, RIVER HAWKBREEZE. SHE IS YOUR SUMMIT BUDDY. YOU'LL SHOW HER AROUND.
HI.
HI.

Professor Willowseed turned to River. "You two have fun with your—"

The wizard's voice fell silent when she looked at Tank. Her old elf eyes darted to me. It was like she saw right through my scales. My throat tightened. I could barely breathe. All I wanted to do was throw off my hood and take a deep gulp of air. Beside me, Tank tugged at the strings of her cloak. Just when I thought I was going to pass out, Professor Willowseed nodded, like she had solved a problem.

"—your new friends, River," she said and shuffled back to the shadow guard. "All right, Flash, do your smoky teleport trick."

The shadow guard nodded. "Certainly, Professor Willowseed."

"Call me Agniz, dear." She took the guard's arm. "'Professor Willowseed' makes me feel old."

The guard started like he'd been gripped by a cave-fisher. "Of course, Mis—er, Agniz."

The cloud of purple smoke reappeared, swallowing Agniz and the shadow guard. The air suddenly returned, and I could breathe again. Beside me, Tank took deep gulps of air. River watched us with her eyebrows raised.

"All right, want to tell me what's really going on?"

"What do you mean?" Aleetha flashed an innocent smile.

"Well, for starters"—River pointed at Tank and me—"those two are not wizards, and they are definitely not elves."

"I told you no one would believe us!" Tank hissed.

"My guess is that you have sneaked them into the Shadow Tower." River walked a circle around us, tapping her thin fingers on her chin as she went. "And that means you are all up to something you don't want anyone else to know about." She stopped and grinned at Aleetha. "Am I right?"

Aleetha's eyes blazed at the elf. "If you must know, we're on the way to the library to visit a friend."

"Sounds exciting!" River said.

"You're not going to report me for sneaking in my friends?"

"No way." River's grin doubled in size. "This trip has been a total bore. But I think all that is going to change."

Aleetha looked to us, her face filled with panic. Her fiery red eyes pleaded for help, but there was nothing Tank or I could do. She sighed and turned to her summit buddy.

"All right, River Hawkbreeze. I hope you like mysteries."

CHAPTER SIX
Magic Vendors and Wood Elves

We had no choice but to tell River the truth.

"I knew it!" she crowed after we'd told her about Professor Lasalan, the robbery at the bookshop and our plan to talk to Mr. Lorof. "I could tell you two weren't wizards. I've never met a goblin and a troll before."

"Well, now you have." Tank smiled.

"And we'd appreciate it if you kept your voice down, so nobody else meets them," Aleetha grumbled.

"Sorry," River said.

"I'm confused," I said. "You don't look like any elf I've ever met before."

"That's because she's a wood elf," Aleetha said.

"We live outside Rockfall Mountain," River said.

"Outside the mountain?" I said. "I've never met someone from outside before."

River grinned. "Well, now you have."

Everyone had heard stories about life outside Rockfall Mountain. Tank's mom always had tales to tell us. She was friends with many ship captains who traveled in and out of Fang Harbor. She had even sailed beyond the harbor and to the world outside when she was younger. Beyond the rocky walls of our mountain, another world existed. If the stories were true, it was a strange place where they did not need glowshrooms in order to see, and monsters like me were not welcome. Seeing River filled my head with more questions than I could count. What was it like outside? How did they live? What was her favorite color?

Before I could ask them, Aleetha led us into a room larger than our school gym and packed with magic, mages and mayhem.

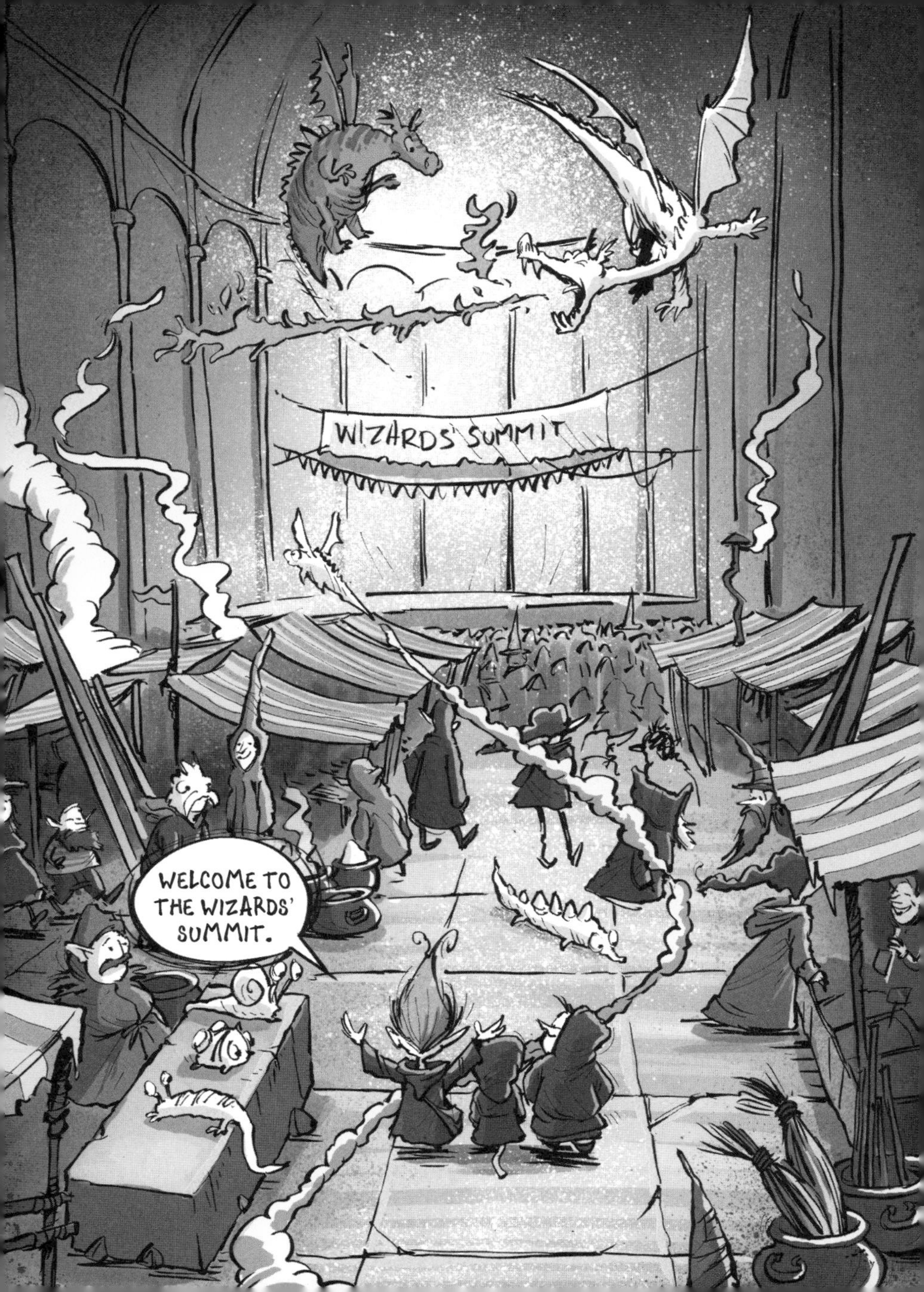
WIZARDS' SUMMIT
WELCOME TO THE WIZARDS' SUMMIT.

"This is the Grand Hall," she said with a sweep of her arms. Every table in the hall held a new magical delight, from fantastic wands and bubbling potions to enchanted scrolls and charmed candles. Clouds of multicolored smoke, bursts of magic-charged light and whoops of wizardy laughter came from each side of the massive room. High above us a pair of shimmering dragons dueled in the air with their fiery breath and deadly claws before vanishing in a puff of purple sparkles. A group of lava elves cheered the mock battle and hurried to buy the illusion stones behind the spell from a grinning rock elf.

"Pretty impressive, huh?" Aleetha smirked. "This is where the school holds graduation ceremonies and stuff. Today it's a vendors' market."

"So the Wizards' Summit is just a big shopping spree for mages?" Tank said with a smirk.

"There are also academic presentations," River said. "My dad is here to give a talk on his research into increasing the range of entanglement-spell effects."

"That sounds suspiciously like school," I said.

Aleetha's eyes went wide. "And who would actually want to learn stuff?"

"You're making fun of me, aren't you?"

Tank chuckled. "Fizz, not everyone is allergic to learning."

"I learn new stuff all the time," I snapped. "Like right now I'm learning how not to run away in panic while surrounded by magic."

Aleetha rolled her eyes. "Keep that in mind as we go through here."

I kept my hood pulled tight and my head down as we hurried through the Grand Hall. Thankfully, we made it to other side without getting attacked by smoke dragons or zapped by magical wands. Aleetha led us out of the ballroom and into a quiet corridor.

We stopped at the bottom of a wide staircase that curved along the wall of the tower.

"The library is several floors up," Aleetha said. "That's where we'll find Mr. Lorof."

We walked up the stairs in silence. Two flights up, River tapped me on my shoulder.

"Your disguise is slipping." She nodded at my tail, now hanging out from under my cloak.

I pulled it back, wrapped it around my belt and wished a cloud of skulls would carry me away again.

"Thanks."

"I always wished I had a tail." She fell into step beside me. "It would be useful for swinging in the trees."

"I've never seen a tree," I said. "Is that really where wood comes from?"

Her eyebrows arched. "You serious?"

"I don't know," I mumbled.

She caught my eye. "Fizz, I'm sorry. I didn't mean anything by that. It's just that everyone knows wood comes from trees."

"I don't. I've never seen a tree. Just the planks that come in on the ships. And even then, the wood gets trucked deep down into the Dark Depths."

River looked around and back down the stairs. "Yeah, nothing around here is made of wood."

"Stones are cheaper," I said. "Trees won't grow down here."

"Of course they won't. There's no sun." She chuckled. "You know—the big ball of fire in the sky?"

I had heard of the sun but had never seen it.

"Is it really made of fire?" I asked.

River shrugged. "That's what they say. You should see it someday."

"I'd like that."

"Hurry up, slowslugs." Aleetha stood beside Tank on the landing, next to a large stone door. The stairs continued up higher in a lazy spiral. The lava elf turned the door's large handle. "Ready to meet Mr. Lorof?"

CHAPTER SEVEN

Flying Sofas and Mr. Lorof

leetha held open the heavy stone door and waved us through.

The wizards' library smelled of gym socks. But that could have just been my feet.

"Don't touch anything," Aleetha whispered. "Some of the books have a nasty bite."

A wall of books curved around us. Floor after floor of shelves packed with thick tomes and dusty scrolls stretched upward as far as I could see. In the middle of the library, overstuffed armchairs and gloom-bean-bags lazily swirled through the air. Footstools and reading lamps drifted past. They rose high into the air on an invisible breeze before slowly drifting downward again.

"Why is all the furniture floating?" Tank asked.

A chesterfield for two sailed past.

"Because it's more fun this way," Aleetha said.

"If you say so." Tank nodded, unconvinced.

"I do," Aleetha said. "Mr. Lorof is upstairs in the history section. Ned found him this morning."

"Ned?" I said. "Who's Ned?"

A few floors above us, an avalanche of books thundered to the ground. It was followed by a mournful wail.

"That's Ned," Aleetha said.

"Your friend sounds hurt," River said.

"I'm sure he's fine. Ned can be a bit clumsy." Aleetha walked to the middle of the room. She spun around to face us. Behind her, flying furniture whooshed by a hair's width from her head. She looked at Tank and then straight at me. "You tech-heads have to trust me. Okay?"

"What do you mean?" Tank narrowed her eyes in suspicion.

"If you want to see Mr. Lorof, you have to follow me." Aleetha stepped back and lifted into the sky.

She rose on a swirling wave of air like an ember from a summer fungi fire.

"That looks like fun." River jumped into the center of the room and flew into the air, whooping with delight.

Tank's ears fell flat against her head.

"I can't do this." Her eyes were wider than a moon-fish's and her skin the color of tired seaweed. "It's magic, Fizz."

"I know, buddy." I took my friend's hand. "But it's Aleetha's magic."

Aleetha whooshed in front of us, riding an orange armchair like a flame surfer from Lava Falls.

"Trust me, Tank," she called before soaring up high into the air.

I didn't like it any better than Tank did. Magic is the one thing monsters like us are meant to avoid. And here we were, right in the heart of it. But it was too late to turn back. We were already too far into the Shadow Tower and too deep into this mystery to stop now. I stepped forward.

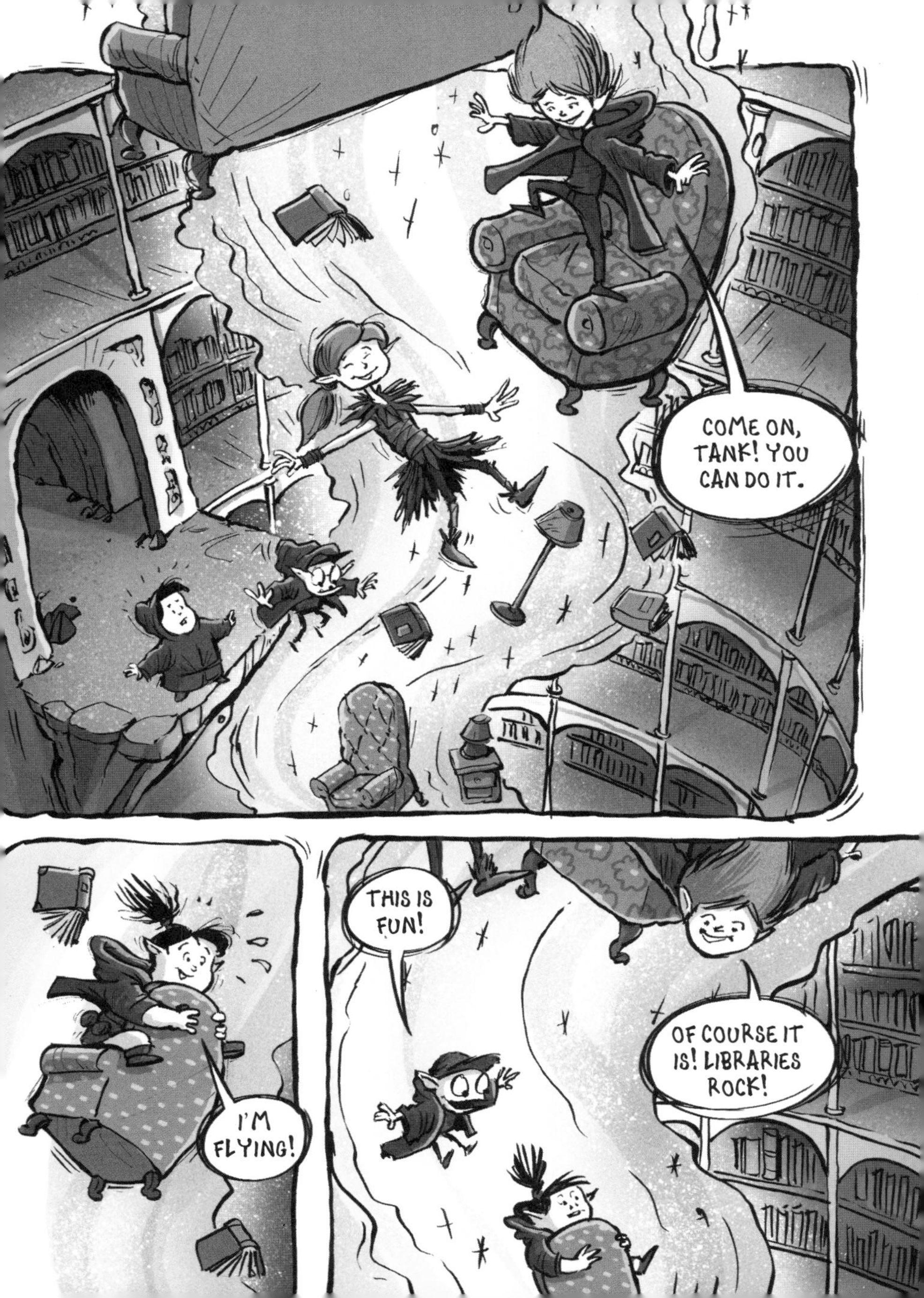
COME ON, TANK! YOU CAN DO IT.
I'M FLYING!
THIS IS FUN!
OF COURSE IT IS! LIBRARIES ROCK!

I was glad to feel solid ground beneath my feet.
Tank landed on the floor with a thud.

"That was interesting," she said, holding her
stomach. "But next time, I'll take the stairs."

"They're fun too." Aleetha shrugged. "But they can
get grumpy if you're wearing heavy boots."

A hand emerged from a pile of books at the end of
an aisle. A head poked out, followed by the rest of an
elf in cloud-lined robes.

"Ned!" Aleetha pulled her friend out of the pile of books. "Are you okay?"

"Yes! Never better." Ned got to his feet and adjusted his glasses. "Just the quantum-ethics manuals having a little fun." The elf turned to the pile of books and wagged his finger. "I just shelved you lot. You cannot be here and on your shelf at the same time!"

I leaned close to Aleetha.

"Why is he talking to a pile of books?"

"Because they never read his notes," Aleetha whispered.

Before I could ask what that even meant, the pile of books vanished.

"And stay there!" Ned shouted across the library floor.

"Where did they go?" Tank asked.

"Where they were all along." Ned scowled at the bookshelves on the far side of the room. "On their own shelf, mucking around with the laws of physics."

"Ned, these are the friends I was telling you about," Aleetha said in a low voice.

Ned's eyes doubled in size. "Ah, yes! I remember." He leaned in to me and whispered, "You're Aleetha's special guests. Don't worry—your true identities are safe with me."

"Thanks, Ned," Aleetha said. "Now, could you show us to your special guest?"

"Of course!" Ned hurried along the aisle. "Follow me! Your friend is this way."

"Nedarius is in some of my classes," Aleetha explained as we walked. "He works part time in the library. I told him about the robbery at Mr. Lorof's bookshop."

"I love visiting that old elf's store." Nedarius stopped in front of a row of shelves stacked with old tomes. "So when I saw him here, I called Aleetha."

HE'S COMING!

DON'T WORRY. WATCH WHAT HE DOES.

POP!

HE VANISHED! WHERE DID HE GO?

HE'S BACK WHERE HE STARTED.

Mr. Lorof slowly floated down the aisle again. He stopped in the exact same spot. Then vanished. He reappeared a second later back where he started. Then he did a repeat performance of the whole routine.

"It's like he's stuck in an endless loop," Tank said. "It happens with technology. Machines do the same thing over and over again until someone turns them off."

"He's been doing this all morning," Ned said.

"Is he a ghost?" I asked.

"In a way," Ned said. "He's trapped in the ghost realm. Real ghosts are not usually this persistent. They do a bit of haunting and then knock off for the day. Mr. Lorof has been at this all morning."

"It would have taken some powerful magic to trap him in the ghost realm." Aleetha watched the ghostly elf walk down the aisle again.

"But it means he is still alive, probably in a deep sleep somewhere," River said. "He needs to be woken soon. If he stays too long in the ghost realm, he'll be trapped there forever."

"Do you think whoever broke into his shop did this to him?" Tank asked.

"I think that's a good guess," Aleetha said.

Mr. Lorof walked down the aisle again. He never took his eyes from the books. He didn't answer when we called his name. He just looped through the same actions over and over.

"Is he looking for something?" Ned asked.

Mr. Lorof stopped, reached up to the bookshelf and vanished once again. That's when it hit me so hard I nearly jumped out of my wizard's cloak.

"He's showing us what we're looking for!" I ran into the aisle and stood in the spot Mr. Lorof stopped at each time. I reached where he reached. My hand hovered in front of a thick book with a black spine and gold letters. "That book! He's showing us that book, but I'm not touching it."

Aleetha pulled the book from the shelf and read the title aloud.

"Domains of Magic: A History of Wizardry."

"Sounds like a yawnfest," I said.

"It's a classic." Ned peered over Aleetha's shoulder as she turned the pages of the thick book. "It explores the history of all the different domains of magic."

Laughter rang out from a floor far below. Ned jolted, sending his glasses sliding off his nose. He caught them and pushed them back into place.

Aleetha closed the book and bolted to the ledge.

"It's Darnan and a couple of second-years," she said.

Ned sighed. "They come here just to goof around. I don't think they've ever cracked open a book here." Something crashed to the floor, followed by more laughter. "They'll be tossing each other into the airlift in a minute."

"We can't let them see Tank and Fizz," Aleetha said. "Fooling adults is one thing, but Darnan knows all the students here. He'll ask questions. Is there another way out of the library?"

"No." Ned grinned. "But I have an idea. Follow me."

He hurried along the edge of the air lift, his cloak fluttering behind him as he went. More laughter came from below. This time it was louder.

"They're floating up here," River said. "And throwing books at each other."

"They are totally losing borrowing privileges," Ned growled.

"I'm sure they'll be heartbroken," Aleetha said.

Ned stopped in front of a large painting hanging on the wall. It showed an old elf in red robes, with wisps of hair peeking out of his ears. Ned tapped the painting several times in a practiced rhythm. The wall slid away to one side, revealing a small dark cubby beyond.

"Hide in here," Ned said. "You'll be safe."

The voices in the air lift grew louder. An elf in a flame-patterned cloak, lounging in an armchair, floated by with his back to us. Tank went in first. I squished in beside her. Ned tapped the painting again. The wall slid closed, plunging us into darkness.

Today had started out with such promise. Now here I was, hiding in the dark from a bunch of wizards. I figured at least things couldn't get any worse. Who knew a goblin could be so wrong?

CHAPTER EIGHT
Lost in Baldur's Bailey

There was barely enough room for my tail.

"You're crushing my foot," I hissed as loudly as I dared. "Move over."

"You move over," Tank snapped back. "We're trapped and surrounded by wizards. This is the worst idea ever."

We were jammed into a dark room no bigger than a closet. Dark, that is, except for two shafts of dim light coming through two small holes in the painting that faced the library. I nudged Tank out of the way and stood on the tips of my claws to look through the holes.

"I can see Aleetha!" I whispered.

"Really?" Tank said. "I bet those holes are the eyes of the monster in the painting! I saw that on TV once." She squeezed in close to see through the holes, but I wasn't sharing.

WELL, IF IT ISN'T ALEETHA CINDERWIMP. THAT LOOKS LIKE A BIG BOOK FOR SUCH A LITTLE MAGE. SURE YOU CAN READ IT?

IT'S CINDERWISP, DARNAN. FLY OFF, OR YOU'LL BE WEARING THIS BOOK AS A HAT.

TOUGH WORDS FROM SUCH A WEAK WIZARD. WATCH IT, OR I'LL TELL INQUISITOR QUANTZ YOU'RE SNOOPING AROUND HERE WHEN YOU SHOULD BE ENTERTAINING OUR WOOD-ELF GUESTS.

STICK A SOCK IN IT, ROCK-HEAD. ALEETHA HAS BEEN VERY WELCOMING. THAT'S MORE THAN I CAN SAY FOR YOU. WHERE IS YOUR SUMMIT BUDDY?

"As student librarian, I can contact other students' mentors." Nedarius waved his hands in front of a glass-ball thing. Whatever it was, it worked on Darnan.

"Fine." The rock elf drifted away from Aleetha and River. "No need to disturb Professor Basalt. You'd better watch it next time or—"

I didn't hear the rest of the rock elf's warning. What I did hear was Tank.

"Ooh, what does this do?" she whispered.

A rush of warm air whooshed down on me from above. The holes in the painting snapped shut. An instant later I felt our little room moving downward.

"What did you do?" I hissed at Tank.

"Nothing!" Her innocent smile collapsed into worry. "Okay, I might have touched this."

Behind her, two small glass balls were stuck into the wall of our hiding spot. One ball was red, and the other was green. The green ball sparkled with magic.

"I…I couldn't resist," Tank stammered. "I know it's magic, but I had to touch the green one to see what it did."

The room shook like it was being hit with sledge-hammers. I steadied myself and glared at my friend.

"Well, now you know," I growled.

Tank ran her hands along the wall. She slipped her zoomers over her eyes.

"It's like an interconnected, weight-displacement mobility system. But powered with magic," she muttered. "Fascinating."

"Stop geeking out!" I snapped. "We are moving in a magic box in a tower of wizards away from the only friend we have. And it's all your fault!"

The room thudded to a stop. The wall slid open again, flooding our hiding spot with light. Another rush of warm air whooshed from behind, pushing us both out of the room. We landed in a heap on the ground in front of our hiding spot. I scrambled to my feet in time to see the wall slide back into place, cutting off any hope of return.

We were back in the plaza surrounding the Shadow Tower. All around us, elves in long cloaks hurried this way and that, chatting, laughing and, thankfully, ignoring two lost monsters in novice cloaks. But we wouldn't be ignored for long. It was only a matter of time before someone noticed Tank's big feet or my tail poking out from our cloaks. Visions of being zapped by shadow guards flashed through my mind.

I threw myself at the wall where the opening had been only seconds ago. I pressed, poked and pounded the hard surface, hoping to trigger whatever it was that would open the secret door. Nothing happened. The dark stone of the Shadow Tower stood firm against my feeble goblin claws.

I spun to face Tank, who still sat on the ground. My scales burned hotter than lava.

"This is all your fault!" I snarled. "You and your button-pushing, lever-pulling curiosity. Why can't you just leave things alone?"

"I'm sorry." Tank sniffed. Her eyes filled with tears. "I couldn't resist. I'm a troll—we're made to tinker. It's in our nature to push buttons. I know it's my fault we've lost Aleetha. Now we'll never find her. And we'll be turned into grubnugs and we'll never get home. I'm sorry."

My curses dried in my mouth. My scales cooled at the sight of my friend blubbering like a kindergartener on the first day of school. I helped Tank to her feet.

"It's okay," I said. "Your button pushing has saved my tail more times than I can remember. We'll find Aleetha again."

Tank dried her eyes with her wizard's cloak. "You really think so?"

"Of course!" I said with as much hope as a goblin surrounded by wizards could muster. "We just have to keep our heads down and act like we belong here. Aleetha said no one will look twice at two novice wizards in this mess of mages."

"You're right," Tank said. She fixed the hood of her cloak to better cover her troll face. "All we have to do is get back into the tower and find the library."

"Easy as failing a math test!"

Tank rolled her eyes. "I wouldn't know." She adjusted my hood so it hid my snout.

"Thanks." I stepped into the crowd of mages. "Now let's find that library."

Many minutes later, we were completely lost.

"Every street looks the same," Tank moaned. "I'm too scared of being spotted to see anything I recognize."

A cloud of black smoke appeared in the middle of the road. Ghostly skulls danced in the smoke as it billowed and grew.

"I recognize that!" I pulled Tank out of the crowd. We hid next to a lava lizard's vending stall.

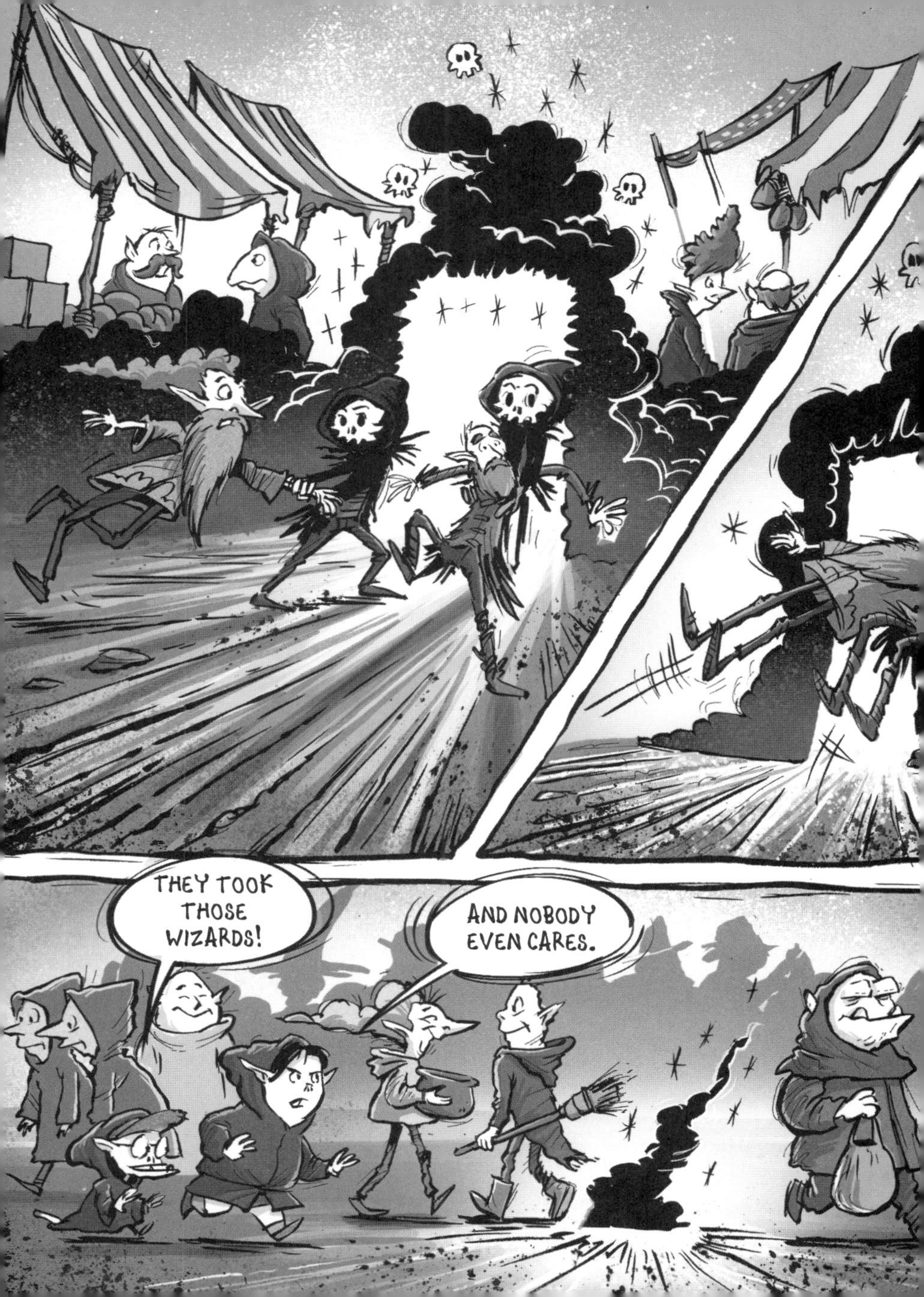
THEY TOOK THOSE WIZARDS!
AND NOBODY EVEN CARES.

CHAPTER NINE
Shadow-Guard Showdown

L ife carried on as usual in Baldur's Bailey.

Not a single elf noticed that two wizards had just been dragged through a magical doorway. Elves of all sizes continued on their way into the summit or shopped at vending stalls for magic supplies.

Tank scratched her ears under her wizard's cloak. "For a bunch of brainy mages, these elves are pretty blind."

"Maybe that's just how things are done here in the Shadow Tower."

"But don't wizards care what happens on their own streets?" Tank pulled her zoomers from her tool belt and slipped them over eyes. "I've got to get a closer look."

She pulled the hood of her cloak over her head, stepped out from our hiding spot and marched into the street.

"Be careful!" I hissed. I followed her into the middle of the road where the wizards had been standing before they were taken. "Remember, we're trying to blend in."

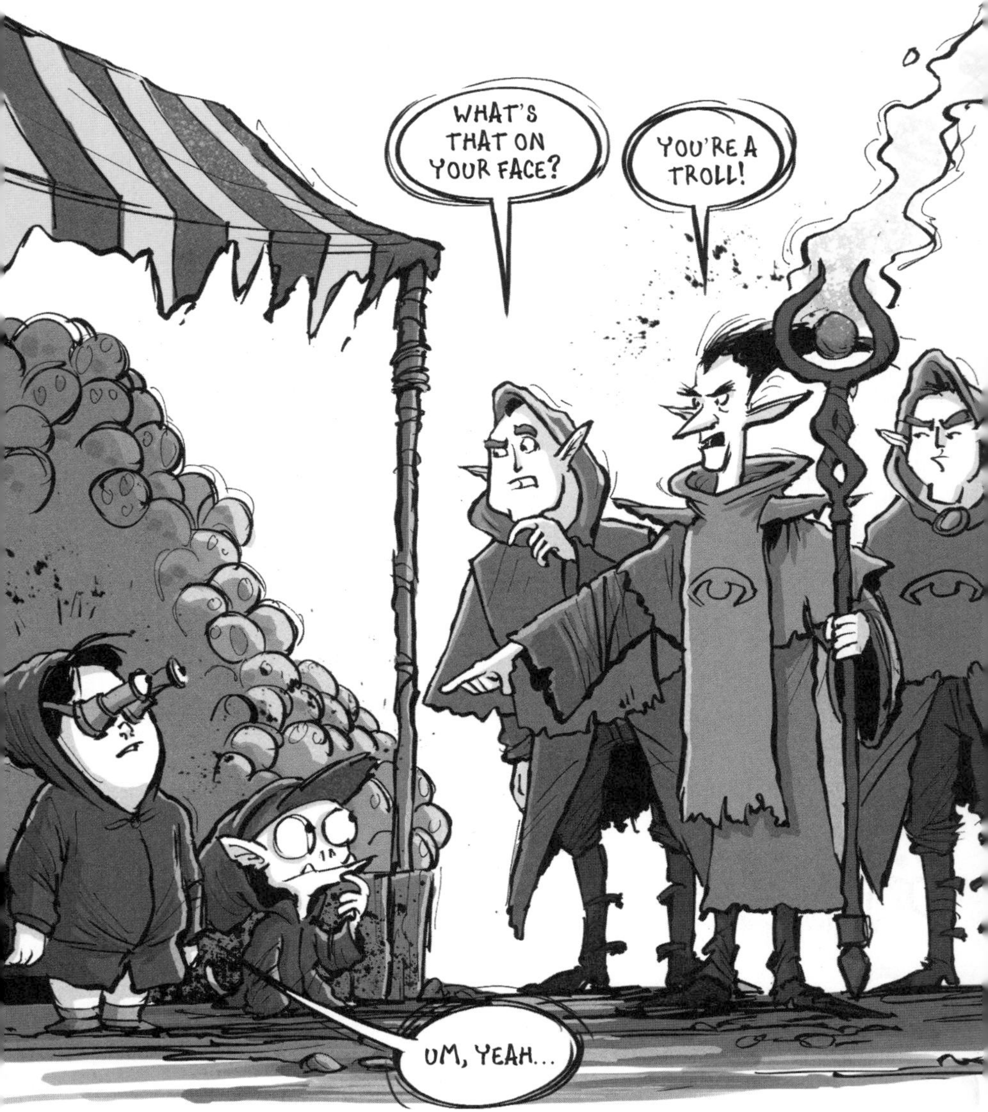
WHAT'S THAT ON YOUR FACE?
YOU'RE A TROLL!
UM, YEAH...

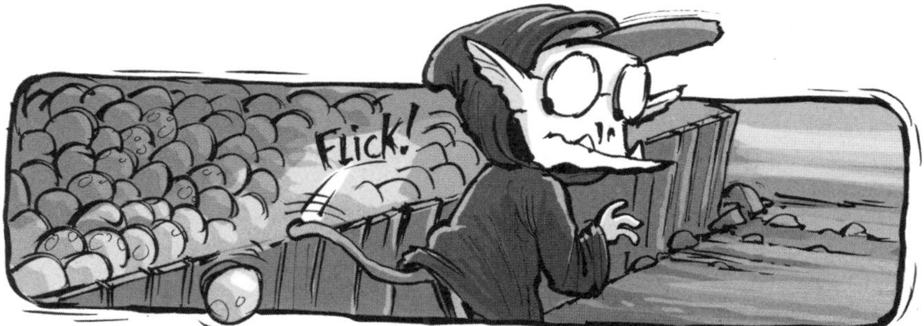
FLICK!

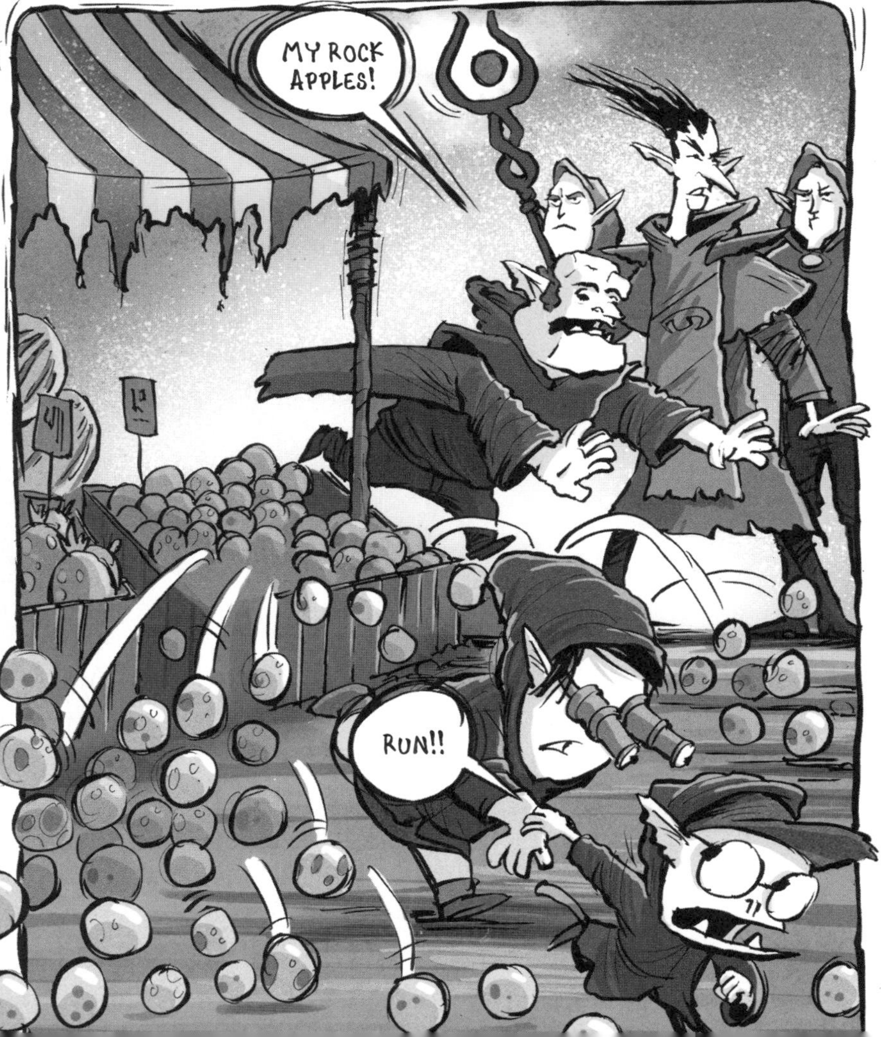
MY ROCK APPLES!
RUN!!

"Stop!" the shadow guards shouted.

We didn't stop. We ran. And so did the guards. I stole a glance over my shoulder to see them pushing their way through the crowd and charging after us.

Tank fell into step beside me. She pulled off the zoomers as she ran but was careful to keep her hood over her head.

"I messed up again! Sorry, Fizz."

"Apologies later," I said. "Running now!"

My tail swung out from under my wizard's cloak as we jumped, ducked and dodged our way through the busy street. I didn't care who saw my scales. I only cared about getting away from those guards before they zapped us with magic. I skipped around a blue-haired elf with her nose in a book and finally saw something familiar.

"The main gates!"

Across the plaza loomed the large iron gates we had sneaked through not so long ago. The entranceway was still jammed with monsters coming and going from the outside. We could slip through and be away from this magic mess. I raced for the gates. I'd had enough of wizards and elves. I wouldn't stop running until I was surrounded by monsters and tech.

"Fizz!"

Or until I heard the voice of our only wizard friend.

From the sea of strangers, Aleetha's face appeared. She pushed through the crowd to where Tank and I were standing. River followed on her heels.

"There you are!" Aleetha wrapped us in a big hug. I was so happy to see her that I didn't complain one bit.

"You found us!" Tank cheered. "I thought we'd lost you for good!"

"We've been searching the entire Shadow Tower," Aleetha said. "We figured you would try to get back to Slick City, so we came to the main gates."

Shouts of protest sounded behind us. The shadow guards pushed through the crowd, roughly checking under the hoods of any wizard about my size.

"Something tells me they're looking for you two," River said.

Tank looked at her feet. "Yeah, that's my bad."

"Shadow guards?" Aleetha stared at the approaching guards in disbelief. "You two have been busy."

"You don't know the half of it," I said.

"Can we chat later? We need to get out of here," River said. "Those guards mean business."

Aleetha grinned. "I know a place those goons won't find us."

CHAPTER TEN
Little Big Spaces

We followed Aleetha away from the main gates and down a narrow street. Crowded shops gave way to small, tumbledown houses packed tightly together. The streets were less busy in this part of the Bailey. Aleetha stopped us where our street met a wider avenue.

"We need to be really careful," she said. "Those guards have probably passed on your descriptions."

"Great! Now we're on the wizards' most-wanted list," Tank moaned.

"Don't panic," Aleetha said. "Just keep your hood up."

"And don't push any more buttons," I hissed to Tank.

"I said I'm sorry about that!" she snapped.

Aleetha stuck her head around the corner. She slowly looked up and down the avenue.

"The way is clear," she said. "Let's go."

We crossed the street in a tight group. I kept my eyes glued to the ground and followed Aleetha. She led us across the avenue and down a twisting path that took us away from the street.

We emerged at an open patch of dusty ground. Stone pillars stood in a circle around the perimeter. They were old and crumbling and more than a little scary.

"Where are we?" I asked.

"This is a magic focal point. They used to have ceremonies here a long time ago." Aleetha walked around the columns, inspecting each one closely. "These columns supported some sort of platform that helped channel the magic energies of this place."

"What happened? Why does no one take care of it?" River spun a slow circle as she took in the ancient structures.

"They built a fancy new focal point at the top of the Shadow Tower." Aleetha shrugged. "Better reception, I guess. Anyway, it means everyone has forgotten about this place."

"We're hiding here?" I scratched my scales and tried not to look scared.

"No, this place is too exposed." Aleetha stopped at a pillar just a little taller than Tank. She tapped the side of the pillar three times. A sparkle of magic ran around the column. A small opening appeared in the stone. "We'll hide in here."

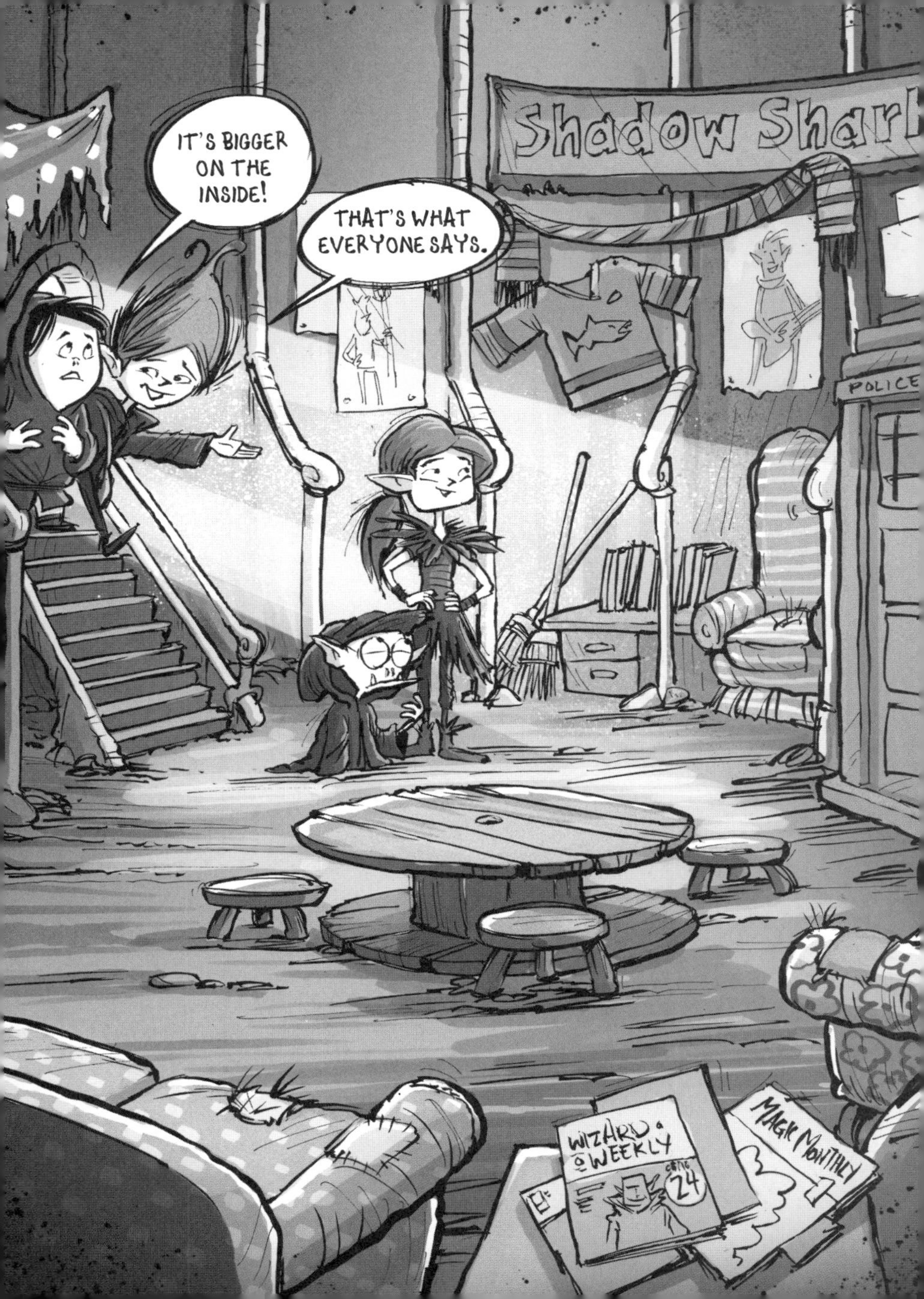
IT'S BIGGER ON THE INSIDE!
THAT'S WHAT EVERYONE SAYS.
Shadow Shar
POLICE
WIZARD WEEKLY
24
MAGIC MONTHLY

My brain hurt just looking at the massive space we had just walked into. From the outside it was just a pillar, but inside there was room for a three-clan goblin hoedown.

"How?" was all I could say.

"What the...?" Tank added, equally confused.

"You shifted the temporal logic essence and realigned the linear space attunements," River said, like she was explaining how to put on a pair of socks.

Tank's jaw hung open. "You made it bigger on the inside."

"You said that already." Aleetha nudged her friend playfully.

"But...that's impossible!" Tank stammered. "It goes against all the laws of engineering."

"This isn't engineering, Tank." Aleetha's grin could not have been wider. "It's magic."

"Very impressive magic," River said.

"Impressive, but not my doing," Aleetha said. "The story is that many years ago a group of fourth-year students conjured this space to play a joke on their mentor. But they never figured out how to reverse the enchantment."

"So it's been here ever since?" I said.

Aleetha nodded. "Yep. The best they could do was wrap it in an attention-deflection charm, so people don't really notice it."

"So to see it, someone has to point it out for you?" River said.

"Exactly." Aleetha flopped into a chair with stuffing popping out of its armrests. "The shadow guards looking for us won't know about this place, so hopefully, we'll be safe here. That is, until some older kids show up. They like to hang out here sometimes."

She rummaged through her satchel and pulled out a thick book that looked familiar.

"Is that the tome from the library? The one Mr. Lorof was trying to get?"

"The very one." Aleetha laid the book on her lap and opened it carefully.

"Nedarius let us borrow it," River said. "Aleetha's had her nose in it ever since."

"No surprise there," Tank called from the other side of the room.

My engineering pal had wandered in a slow circle around the hiding spot, touching the walls, still unable to make sense of it all. I, on the other hand, didn't even try to understand. I do love solving mysteries, but when it comes to magic, it's better to just accept what you see and move on.

"I think I know why Mr. Lorof's ghost was looking for it." Aleetha thumbed through the pages, searching for something.

"At first we couldn't figure out why it was special," River said.

Aleetha stopped paging through the book.

"And then we found this," she said.

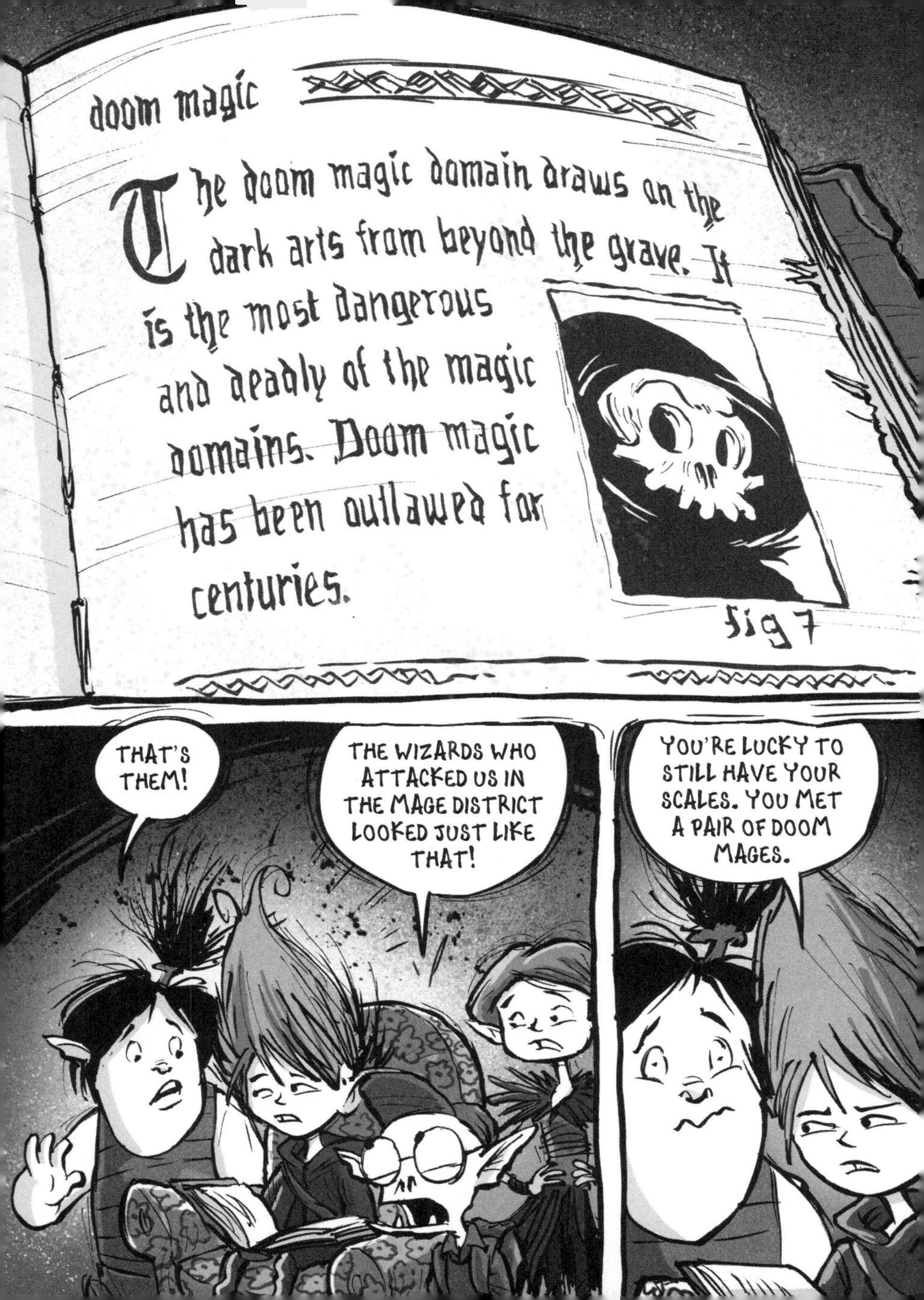
doom magic
The doom magic domain draws on the dark arts from beyond the grave. It is the most dangerous and deadly of the magic domains. Doom magic has been outlawed for centuries.
fig 7
THAT'S THEM!
THE WIZARDS WHO ATTACKED US IN THE MAGE DISTRICT LOOKED JUST LIKE THAT!
YOU'RE LUCKY TO STILL HAVE YOUR SCALES. YOU MET A PAIR OF DOOM MAGES.

"I disagree," River said. "Doom magic was banned a long time ago. There haven't been doom mages for centuries."

"The black cloaks are returning!" Aleetha bolted upright, nearly knocking the book to the floor.

"That's what your mentor said in her message," Tank said.

"Professor Lasalan knew the doom mages were returning. That's why she sent us that warning."

"I don't believe it." River crossed her arms. "They can't just suddenly reappear from nowhere."

"Wanna bet?" I said. "Tank and I have seen them. Twice."

Aleetha looked up from the book. "What do you mean twice?"

"We saw those skull-faces steal a forest mage and a wind mage right in the middle of the street!" Tank tugged at her tool belt like someone had filled its pouches with itching powder.

"And no one even did anything!" I told them about the magical doorway appearing and the doom mages dragging the wizards back through the portal before it vanished. "Everyone just kept walking by, chatting and laughing. It was like no one even cared."

"Or no one saw," River said.

"How could that be?" Tank gave her belt another firm tug. "It happened in the middle of a busy street."

"There are spells in forest magic that can obscure reality for a short time. Make others not notice what is right in front of them."

"Just like the enchantment on this place," Aleetha said.

"But Tank and I saw everything," I said. "We noticed what was in front of us."

River tapped her chin with a long finger. "Yes, that's the bit that has me confused."

Tank flopped into a chair and let out a long sigh. "Everything in this place has me confused."

I had to admit, this case had my brain aching too. Why had the doom mages returned? Where had they come from? Why were they stealing mages? And, most important, why didn't I bring any cookies with me? Cracking a case goes much faster with a plate of choco-slug supremes at your side.

"It says here that small groups of doom mages still exist but keep their true identity a secret." Aleetha read aloud: *"A small army of doom mages may be hiding in plain sight, posing as mages from other domains, waiting for the return of the Doom Master."*

"Doom Master? Who is that?" Tank said before I could.

"This is too big for us," River said. "We should talk to the shadow guard."

"We can't yet," Aleetha said. "If they found out I snuck a goblin and a troll into the Shadow Tower, I'd get expelled from the Shadow Tower."

"All right," River said. "But we need to find an answer quickly. Three mages are already missing, and we don't know why."

"Maybe the why isn't important right now," Tank said. "Maybe we should be asking who is next? They've taken three wizards in the last two days. Are they finished? Will they take another mage?"

"Brilliant, Tank!" Aleetha was on her feet, book in hand, and pacing quickly around the room. "They have taken mages from fire, air, water and forest domains of magic."

"That leaves stone domain," River said. "We need to warn them. We must tell Agniz."

"Your mentor?" I gulped. That old wood elf seemed nice. But it also seemed like she could see through my disguise.

River turned to Aleetha. "We won't tell her about Tank and Fizz."

Aleetha nodded. "That could work, if you guys stay out of sight."

"Yeah, we've done really well at that so far." Tank rolled her eyes.

"Why can't we just stay here?" I asked. "And you come back after talking to your mentor?"

"Because a bunch of upper-year students could come in." Aleetha arched her eyebrows. "Then what would you do?"

"Um, stay out of sight?"

"That settles it," Tank said. "We're going with you."

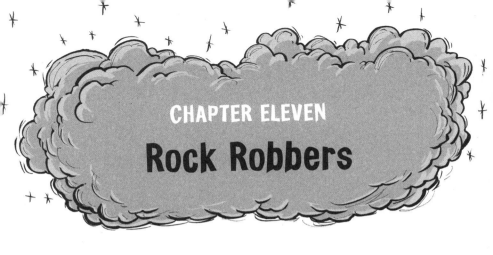

CHAPTER ELEVEN
Rock Robbers

Agniz Willowseed knew how to command a crowd. The old wood elf stood in front of a packed room of wizards. Tank and I stayed at the back, hoods pulled over our heads. River and Aleetha sat with the other wizards near the front. Agniz had the mages hanging on her every word. She slammed her large staff on the floor to drive home her point. The staff had a ring of green leaves at the top and ended in a gnarl like an old wortbeast. The thud echoed throughout the room. I jumped. It happens.

"In conclusion, we must all work harder to ensure that only high-quality spell ingredients are used at all times!"

Mages from every domain cheered as Agniz bowed to their applause. Chancellor Rund walked to the front of the room and stood beside Agniz.

"Thank you, Agniz, for your wise words." Chancellor Rund turned to the crowd. "That concludes this session. Thank you all for coming."

The gathered wizards got up from their seats and filed out of the room. Aleetha and River went to Agniz and Chancellor Rund.

"Agniz!" River said to her mentor. "We need your help."

"What ever is the matter, dear?" Agniz said.

River and Aleetha told Agniz and Chancellor Rund about the mages being taken, Professor Lasalan's warning and the coming of the doom mages.

THAT'S BECAUSE THEY CAN'T SEE IT.

THE DOOM MAGES ARE USING A SPELL THAT HIDES THEM.

MISSING WIZARDS AND DOOM MAGES? YOUNG ELVES SHOULD NOT WORRY ABOUT SUCH TERRIBLE THINGS.

IF THE DOOM MAGES WERE HIDDEN, HOW DID YOU SEE THEM?

WE DIDN'T. OUR FRIENDS DID.

BUT THEY'RE NOT HERE RIGHT NOW.

Agniz and Chancellor Rund looked at each other.

"I see," the chancellor said. But it was clear she did not see.

I wanted to jump on my seat at the back of the room and shout that my friends were telling the truth. But that would ruin the whole staying-out-of-sight thing.

Chancellor Rund sighed. "I'm sure your missing wizards will return very soon."

Aleetha was not ready to give up.

"But Mr. Lorof has disappeared too!" she said. "Professor Lasalan has still not returned from her research trip into the Depths. And she sent us a warning message."

"Ah, Professor Lasalan is always late." Chancellor Rund smiled. "And she is always spreading messages of doom and gloom. Last month she sent letters to the whole council pleading with us to save the spotted lava skunk from extinction. I mean, who could be bothered saving a smelly lava skunk?"

"Perhaps we should warn the shadow guard, just in case?" Agniz said.

"I suppose." Chancellor Rund shrugged. "I will speak to Inquisitor Quantz. He is in charge of the shadow guard. He will tell them to watch out for suspicious elves in dark cloaks."

"There, problem solved." Agniz smiled at Aleetha and River. "Now run along. I'm sure you have more exciting things to do than worry about a few forgetful wizards."

"But—" River's protest was cut short by Agniz's sharp look.

"Run along, River."

Agniz turned to Chancellor Rund and began talking as though they weren't even there.

River and Aleetha retreated out of the room.

"Well, that was a waste of time," River grumbled. "They didn't even take us seriously. We need to talk to the boulder mages." River turned to Aleetha. "Do you know any rock elves?"

"Just one." Aleetha sighed. "And he's a jerk."

Darnan blocked our path.

"No way am I letting you disturb Professor Basalt." The rock elf planted his large feet into the ground in front of the doorway to the rock elves' chambers.

"Don't be a bigger rock-head than you already are, Darnan." Aleetha scowled. "It will only take a minute."

"It's important," River said. "Professor Basalt is in danger. What we have to say could help him and all rock elves."

Darnan smirked. "Rocks don't need any help from silly wood or lava elves. Run along and try not to burn yourself."

Flames ran along Aleetha's cloak at Darnan's words. For a second I thought she'd turn the rock elf into a campfire. River placed a hand on her friend's shoulder and said something in a language I didn't understand. The flames wicked away to nothing as calm returned to the lava elf.

Tank and I watched all of this unfold from our hiding spot. We were both crammed into a narrow doorway down the hall, far from the rock elves' chambers. The walls and floors in this part of the Shadow Tower were smooth and polished to a shine. We were high in the tower, above the library and the commotion of the Wizards' Summit. This floor was reserved for the rock elves and their out-of-town visitors. Monsters like us were not welcome.

It took all my strength not to charge out and whack Darnan on his big rocky head. Tank's arms holding me back helped too.

"Relax, Fizz," she whispered to me. "Aleetha can handle it."

"I know," I growled. "I'm just tired of watching bullies be bullies."

"This bully can turn you into a pile of pebbles, so stay out of it."

"We don't have time," I muttered. "Aleetha and River need to warn Professor Basalt that boulder mages are next on the 'let's steal a wizard' list before those skull-faces strike again."

The door behind Darnan swung open slowly and silently. He jumped to attention and hurried Aleetha and River out of the way. A large rock elf wearing a high-collared wizard's cape stepped into the hallway, like a mountain on the move.

"Professor Basalt!" Aleetha called.

"We have an urgent message for you, sir!" River added.

Darnan stood in front of the elves with his arms spread wide, blocking them from getting any closer.

"I'm sorry, sir," Darnan said. "I told them to leave, but they refuse to listen."

Professor Basalt stopped his march and slowly turned his massive head to look down on Aleetha and River.

"I am far too busy, and too important, to listen to a pair of children."

"This isn't going well," Tank whispered.

The air at the far end of the corridor shimmered. My scales started itching like I'd rolled on a nest of fangnits. A black cloud of smoke grew from nowhere, only a few steps away from the arguing elves. A doorway appeared.

"It's about to get a lot worse," I hissed.

Two skull-faces in black cloaks walked out of the doorway within reach of the elves. They moved silently closer.

"Why aren't they freaking out?" Tank hissed. "Can't they see those doom mages?"

"Nope!" I wriggled free of Tank's grip. "Only we can see them!"

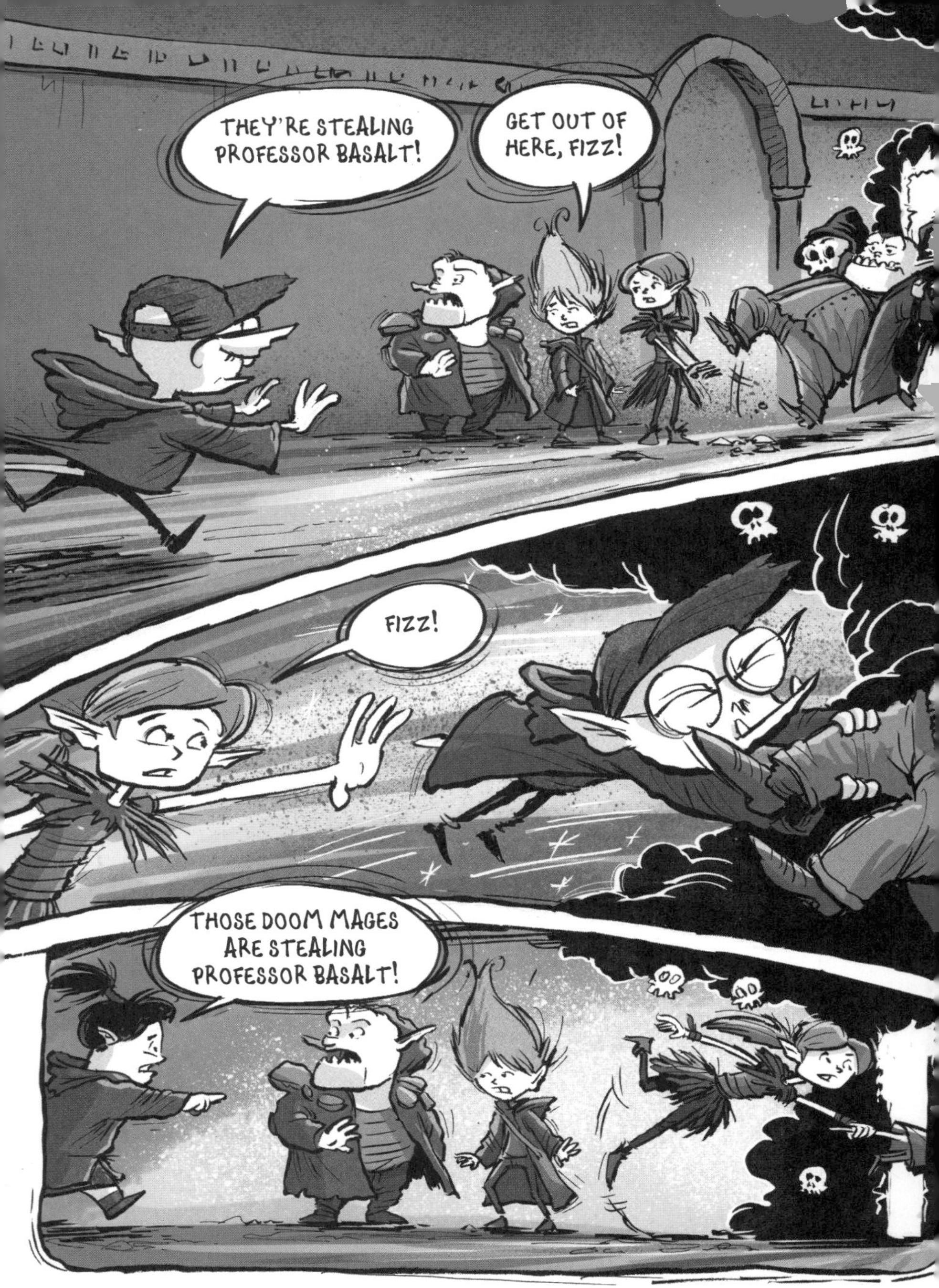
THEY'RE STEALING PROFESSOR BASALT!
GET OUT OF HERE, FIZZ!
FIZZ!
THOSE DOOM MAGES ARE STEALING PROFESSOR BASALT!

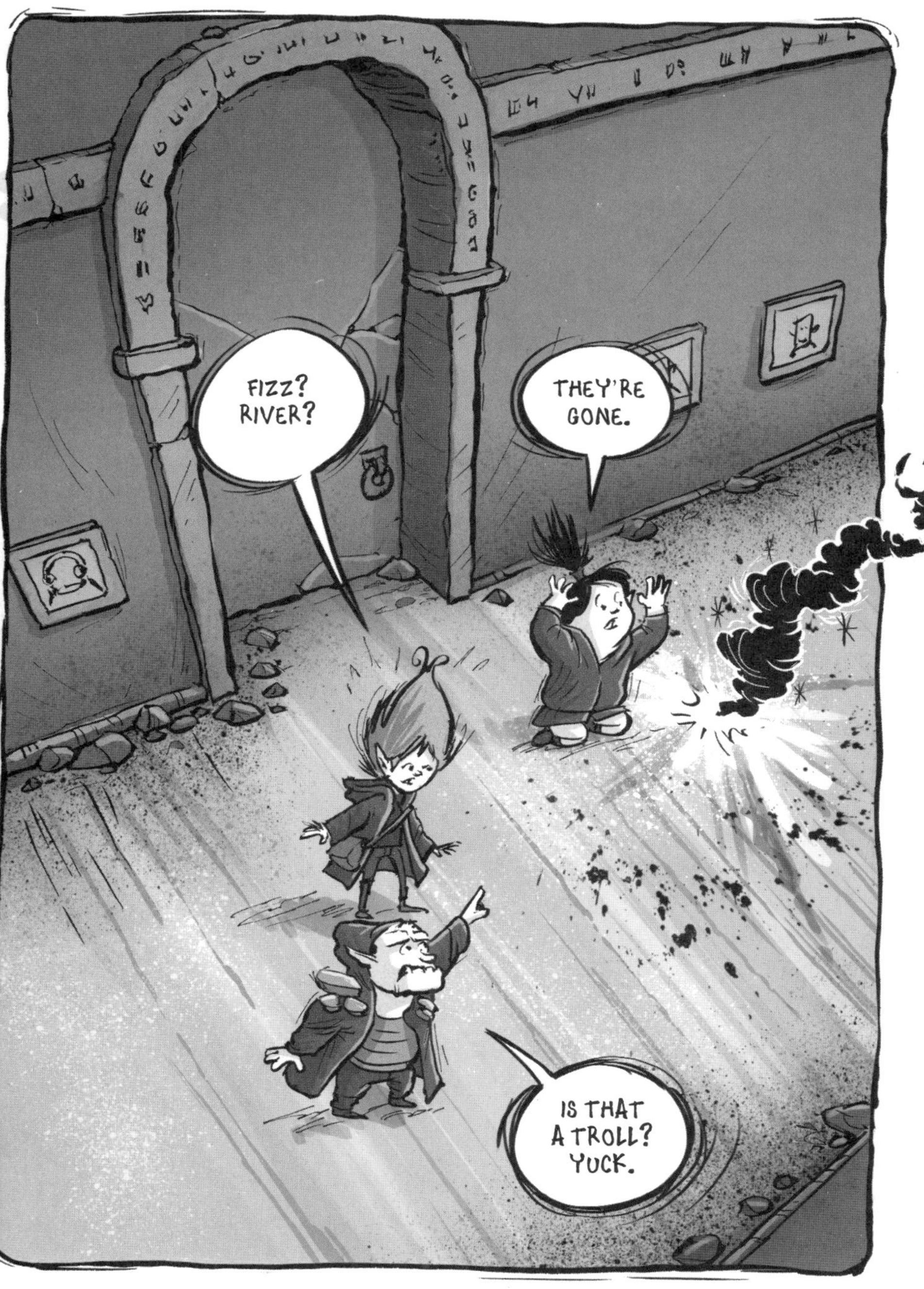
FIZZ? RIVER?
THEY'RE GONE.
IS THAT A TROLL? YUCK.

CHAPTER TWELVE
Enter the Doom Master

Getting smashed through a magic doorway with two doom mages and a rock elf the size of a mountain really puts a dent in your scales.

We landed in a heap with me at the bottom. I couldn't move. It felt like all of Slick City was standing on my back. I wished for the millionth time that I had stayed in bed. My head felt like a mudball on sports day. My tail ached as though someone had used it as a jump rope. But my ears were working just fine.

"This one is heavy," said a voice above me.

"That is why we saved him for last," another voice answered. "Hurry up. We don't want to keep Master waiting."

Their words came out in a low hiss, like they were talking through one of Tank's phone contraptions. The pair of doom mages grunted, and the weight was suddenly lifted from my back. I cracked open one eye to see them helping Professor Basalt to his feet.

The boulder mage wobbled like he'd been on the wrong end of a mudball tournament too. The doom mages took him by the arms and led him through an open doorway. I stayed still long after they had vanished into the shadows beyond the room.

"You can get up now." Another voice. This one was familiar.

"River! How did you get here?" The wood elf helped me to my feet. The room danced like a toddler on roller skates. "Wherever here is."

River held me steady and smiled. "I hitched a ride on your tail, and then I zapped you with a camouflage spell. Your head will clear up very soon."

"That explains why those skull-faces didn't see me." The walls around me slowed their dance to a shuffle. My head started to clear. "And nobody saw them when they attacked Professor Basalt."

"I only saw them when you and Tank came charging at us," River said. "They were using a spell to hide themselves. Agniz taught me one very similar. The shock of seeing you two snapped me out of the spell's effects."

"That's just like when Tank and I saw them take those wizards," I said. "They snatched them from a busy street and nobody except me and Tank saw anything."

"Maybe trolls and goblins are too smart to be fooled by a hiding spell?" River said.

"I like how you think."

"We need to warn the shadow guard." She looked around the room and sighed. "But first we have to figure out where we are."

Now that my vision had returned, I saw we were in a small room filled with cloaks. Along the walls stood several cloak racks, holding cloaks of many colors and sizes. The only way out was the doorway the doom mages had just gone through.

"We are either in a very large closet or the back room of a cloak shop," I said.

"Or on top of the world," River said.

She had pushed aside a rack and now stood in front of a small window.

I stepped back from the window. The walls were wobbling again, but this time it wasn't the effects of a spell.

"But only the most senior wizards are allowed at the top of the tower," River said. "They don't allow apprentices like me in here."

"And they definitely don't allow goblins," I said. "We need to get out of here and back to Aleetha."

River peered out the doorway. "The corridor is empty. There should be stairs along here somewhere."

"Let's find them before we get found." I pulled my hood over my head and joined River at the door.

We slipped into the hallway. With every step a new question formed in my brain.

"How can a bunch of doom mages be in the Shadow Tower?" I asked. "I thought doom magic had been outlawed."

"It has," River said. "Someone is hiding something."

"Like a body," I said.

I stood in the doorway of a small room with a single bed. In the bed was an elf. An old and familiar elf.

"Mr. Lorof!" I ran to the old bookseller's side. His eyes were closed, and he didn't move.

"Is he…you know…" River let her words trail off.

The bed covers moved up and down slowly.

"No," I said. "He's in a deep sleep. Very deep. And he's still trapped in the ghost realm."

River nodded. "We might be able to wake him with some thistle-wine soup. Brewed in a hemlock grove at midnight is best."

"We don't have thistles or hemlock groves, whatever they are. Even if we did, I wouldn't have the first clue about where to find them."

"Pepper granite works well too," River said. "I'm sure you have plenty of that down here. You just have to mine it, grind it and boil it into a potion. That stuff will wake the dead."

"Too bad I left my pickax, grinder and potion-making kit at home."

"I'm only trying to help," River snapped.

"I'm sorry. All this magic is getting to me." I shook Mr. Lorof gently, but he was out like a first-grader after a long field trip. "We need to wake him."

Footsteps echoed in the hallway outside the little room. We both ducked behind the door and held our breath. At least, I held mine.

Two shadows crossed the doorway, one after the other. We waited in silence for a moment, and then River stuck her head out into the corridor.

"Professor Thornwise!" River whispered. "He's with a doom mage."

I poked my head out in time to see them step into a room farther down the dark hall. "That's the guy I saw get taken earlier!"

River was on her feet the moment they were gone.

"Where are they going?" She hurried after them.

"Wait!" I jumped to my feet and ran to catch up with her. "Where are you going?"

"To get some answers."

She stopped at the doorway Professor Thornwise and the doom mage had just walked through. No light came from the other side. A wall of shimmering blackness filled the opening, sparkling with an energy that chilled me to the tip of my tail.

"Magic." I gulped.

"What else did you expect in the Shadow Tower?"

Footsteps sounded in the corridor from the way we had just come.

"Someone is coming!" I hissed.

River took my arm. "Then let's get going."

She pulled me through the doorway.

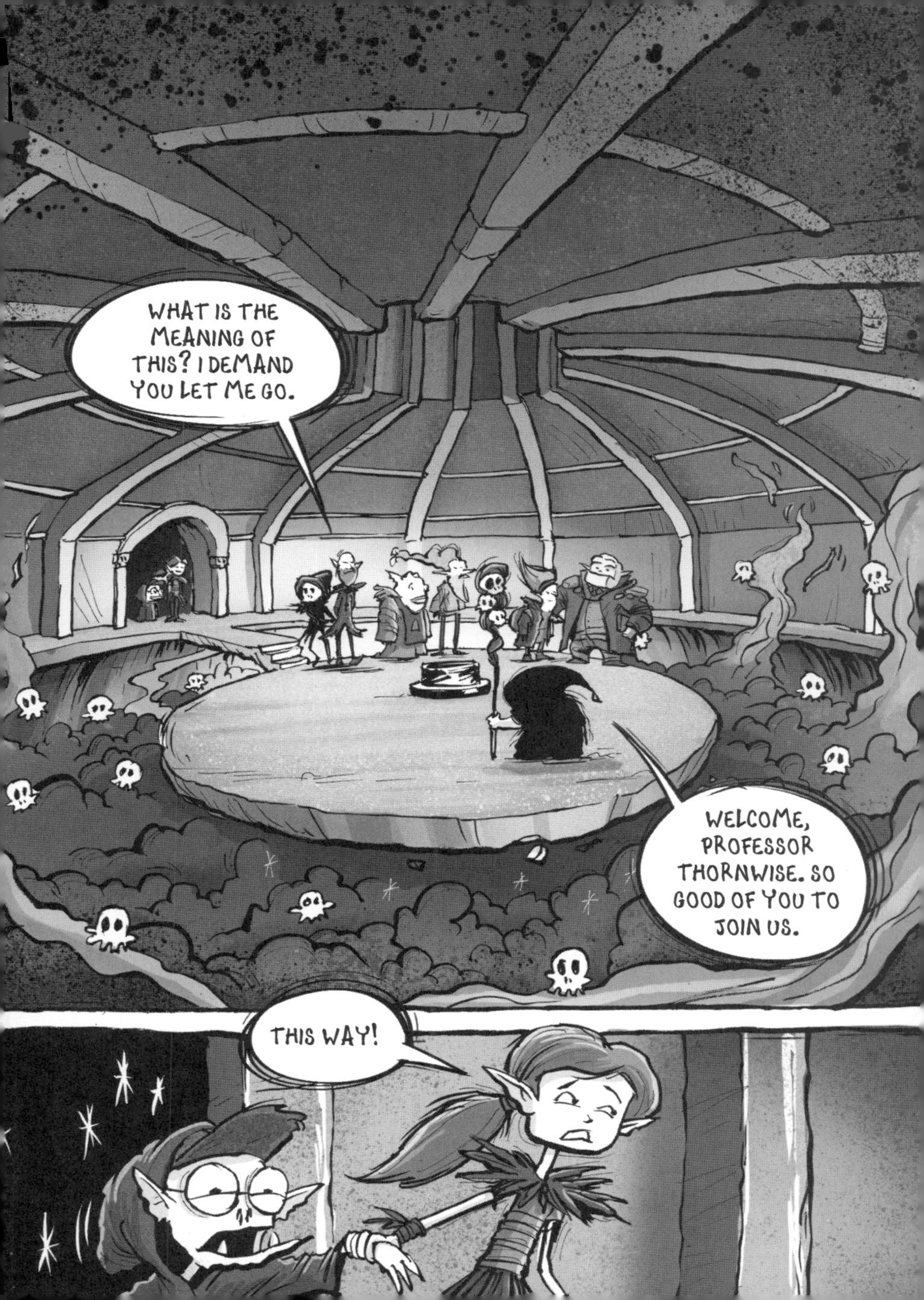
WHAT IS THE MEANING OF THIS? I DEMAND YOU LET ME GO.
WELCOME, PROFESSOR THORNWISE. SO GOOD OF YOU TO JOIN US.
THIS WAY!

I dove into the corner next to River. We wrapped our cloaks around us and huddled in the shadows. Dread seeped under my scales, but I forced myself to peer out from under my hood.

The room was doom-mage central. Dark magic wafted up from the floor and swirled around the chamber like a heavy fog drifting in from Fang Cove. In the middle of the room stood a pedestal of dark stone on a circular platform. Around the pedestal, three mages waited in perfect stillness, their faces blank and staring.

My heart leaped into my throat at the sight of the wizards. The elf nearest us was a wave mage. Beside him was the cloud elf I saw taken away with Professor Thornwise. Across the platform stood a third elf, the wizard we'd been looking for since the beginning of this mess.

"Professor Lasalan!" I whispered.

Aleetha's mentor stood less than a dozen hops away from us, but I was miles away from solving this mystery. Like the others, Professor Lasalan remained unmoving and silent.

The doom mage from the corridor pushed Professor Thornwise into position beside the other wizards.

"Unhand me this instant!" Professor Thornwise pushed away the doom mage's arm. He spun to face the smaller doom mage behind the pedestal. His eyes grew wide. "The Staff of Skulls! It can't be."

"You recognize your old nemesis, Professor Thornwise?" The small doom mage held the massive staff into the air. "It seems all your work to destroy this staff was for nothing."

"I don't know how you got that staff, but you must destroy it." Thornwise struggled against his captor but could not break free. "You won't get away with this!"

"I'm afraid I will, Professor." The small doom mage chuckled and pointed the staff at the wood elf.

A ghostly light enveloped the staff. A bone-white skull shot out from the staff and collided with Professor Thornwise before vanishing like smoke into the darkness. Professor Thornwise fell silent and stood suddenly still. He stared out in front of him with an empty gaze, just like the other mages.

Two more figures stepped through the shimmering doorway and into the room. Professor Basalt pulled against the doom mage that held his arm.

"Let go of me! Do you know who I am?" the rock elf barked. Despite his large size, he could not break free from the doom mage's grip.

"Welcome, Professor Basalt," said the small doom mage. "You are the last of my guests to arrive."

Basalt glared at the doom mage with the large staff. "I am not your guest. I don't even know who you are!"

"How rude of me," said the doom mage. "You may call me the Doom Master."

"I will do no such thing!" Basalt thundered.

My tail nearly snapped with fear. The Doom Master, leader of the doom mages, was in the same room, and I had only the shadows to hide me.

The Doom Master pointed the staff at Professor Basalt. A ghostly skull shot from the staff and wrapped around the boulder mage. When it had drifted away to nothing, Professor Basalt stood still and silently stared ahead.

"Much better," the Doom Master said. "Move the rock-head into place."

The doom mage obeyed the command and walked Professor Basalt to stand near the pedestal. All five wizards stood as still as statues, facing the pedestal.

"Prepare yourselves, professors of the Shadow Tower." The Doom Master lay the staff across the pedestal.

"You have the honor of becoming the first in a new order of wizards. You will spread the power of the skull to all mages in your domain. And from there, we will conquer Rockfall Mountain."

The sound of grinding stone boomed from the darkness above. From our hiding spot, River and I watched as the roof directly above the pedestal slid open like a window. A shaft of pale light shot through the hole and washed over the staff resting on the pedestal. The staff hummed like one of Tank's machines powering up.

"Is that moonlight?" River whispered.

Before I could ask what in the name of slick she was talking about, shafts of pale light burst out from the staff and straight at each of the stunned wizards. Five beams of eerie light shot directly into the faces of the five mages.

"It begins!" the Doom Master crowed.

The light engulfed each mage's head until it was so bright I could not watch anymore. Then, as suddenly as it had come, the light vanished from the staff. The wizards remained standing, but they had not escaped unchanged. Gone were their silent and still faces. In their places were the sinister skulls. On their backs hung the black cloaks marking them as doom mages.

The Doom Master retrieved the staff from the pedestal. High above us, the roof rumbled closed, and the room was plunged into darkness once again.

"Whom do you serve?" demanded the Doom Master.

As one, the most powerful wizards in Rockfall Mountain responded. "We serve the skull. We serve the Doom Master!"

"As will all wizards in the Shadow Tower!" The Doom Master thrust the staff into the air. "By the Staff of Skulls, the Army of Doom will return!"

River gasped at the sight of the skull-faced mages. And that was all it took to doom us.

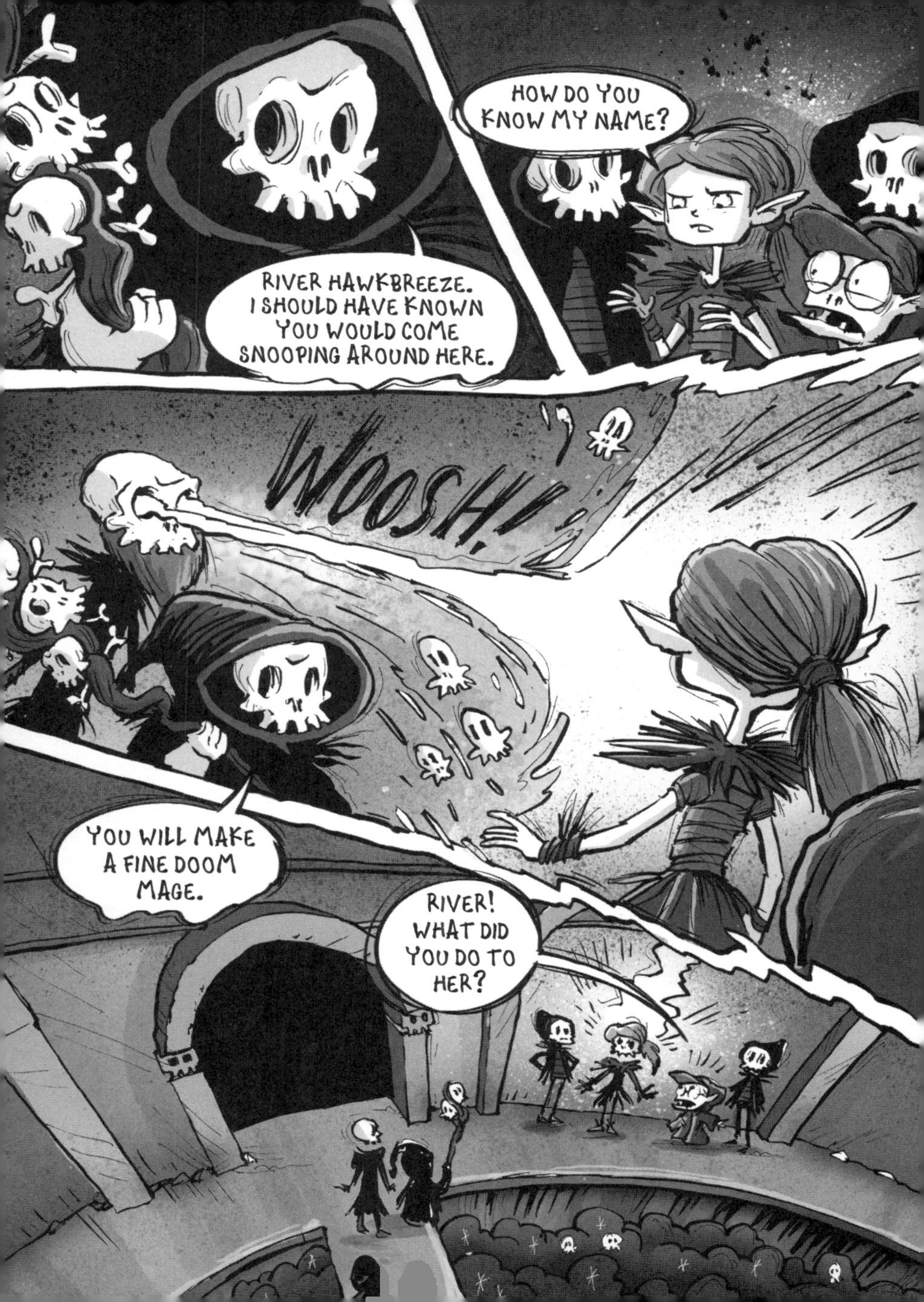
RIVER HAWKBREEZE. I SHOULD HAVE KNOWN YOU WOULD COME SNOOPING AROUND HERE.
HOW DO YOU KNOW MY NAME?
WOOSH!
YOU WILL MAKE A FINE DOOM MAGE.
RIVER! WHAT DID YOU DO TO HER?

The world exploded in a blast of skulls. Soul-crushing, mountain-heavy dread gripped me. I felt myself falling. Then everything went dark.

CHAPTER THIRTEEN
Ghost-Realm Refuge

"Wake up, Sonny!"

Fog soaked my brain. Pain scorched my scales. I felt like I'd stuck my tail in one of Tank's machines. A face pushed through the fog. It was wrinkled, blurry and completely gray. An equally gray arm reached out and helped me to my feet.

"Easy there, little goblin." The stranger held my elbow as the world swirled around me.

"Am I alive?"

"You could say that." The elf chuckled. He had wild hair and tiny glasses and was gray from head to toe, but he wasn't wearing a wizard's cloak. I recognized him immediately.

"Mr. Lorof!"

"The very one." Mr. Lorof bowed. "It seems I found you just in time."

"Found me?" I said. "River and I found you. You were asleep at the top of the tower. When we saw you in the library, you were a ghost."

That's when I noticed my arms. They were gray like Mr. Lorof. And they weren't alone. My legs, claws and tail were completely gray too, like someone had squeezed out all my wonderful green. My stomach felt like it was being sucked down the drain.

"I'm a ghost too."

"Something like that," Mr. Lorof said.

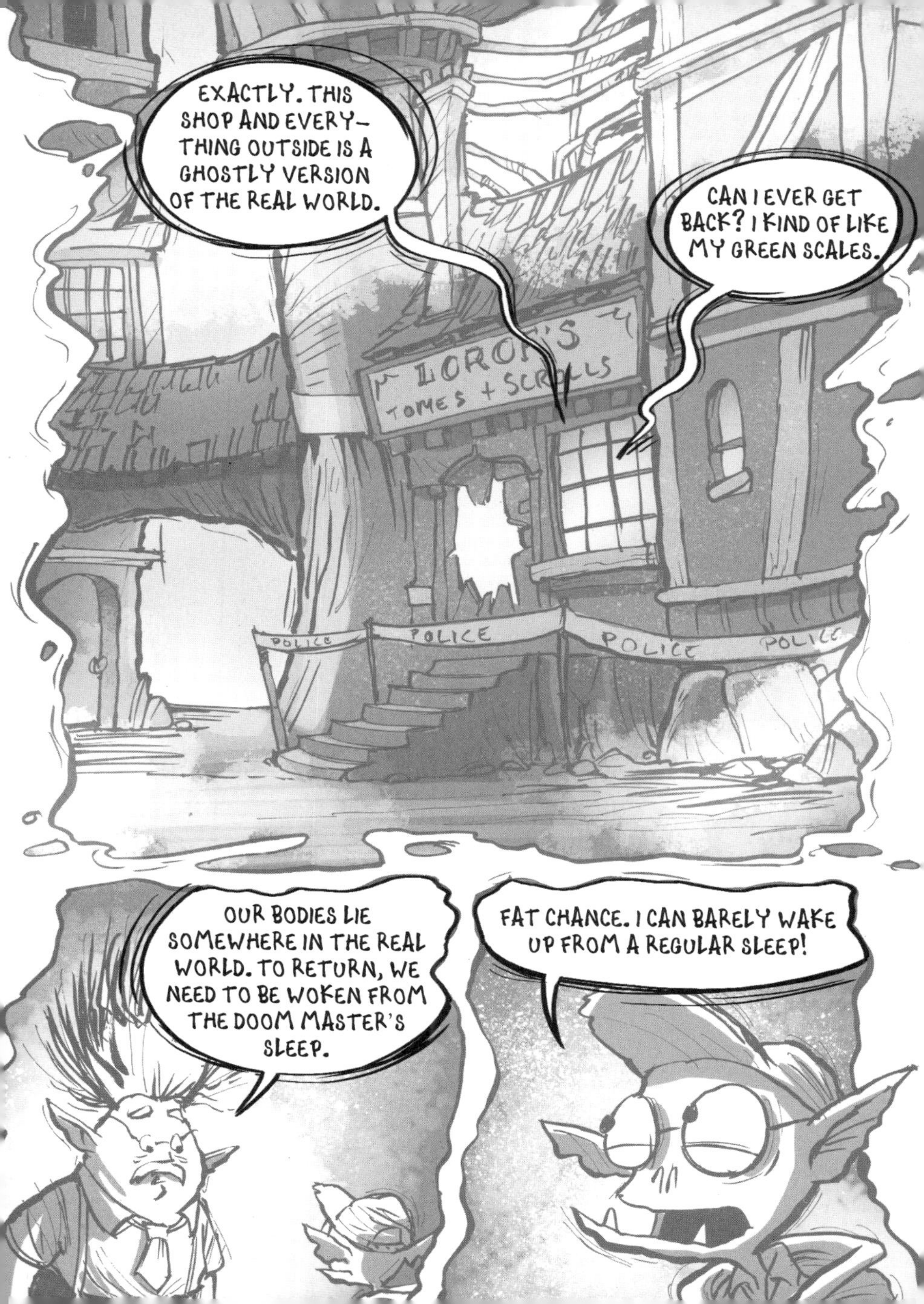
EXACTLY. THIS SHOP AND EVERY-THING OUTSIDE IS A GHOSTLY VERSION OF THE REAL WORLD.
CAN I EVER GET BACK? I KIND OF LIKE MY GREEN SCALES.
OUR BODIES LIE SOMEWHERE IN THE REAL WORLD. TO RETURN, WE NEED TO BE WOKEN FROM THE DOOM MASTER'S SLEEP.
FAT CHANCE. I CAN BARELY WAKE UP FROM A REGULAR SLEEP!

Gray misty light streamed in through the windows lining the front wall of the room. Beyond the windows, it was as gray as Fang Harbor on a foggy morning.

"Professor Lasalan's message told us to warn you about the black cloaks returning," I said. "She thought you would know what to do. But we got here too late. They had already taken you."

"All will be well, Fizz," Mr. Lorof said. "We'll figure out a way to get back. I've been watching those doom mages. I saw what they did to you and brought you back here to safety." The elf's eyes twinkled. "I might not be a wizard but I do know a thing or two about magic."

Mr. Lorof's words calmed my spinning stomach. I was alive, sort of. That was better than being dead, any day of the week. And it was better than getting turned into a skull-face. I bolted upright at the thought.

"River! She was with me. She's a forest mage. The Doom Master turned her into one of those skull-faces." The image of a skull floating around River wafted through the fog in my brain. "The Doom Master is going to turn all the wizards into doom mages. Then they're going to take over the Shadow Tower."

"That is what I feared." Mr. Lorof sighed. "The Doom Master chose those wizards for a reason."

"Each wizard was from a different domain," I said.

"Good observation," Mr. Lorof said. "I can see why you're a good detective. There's more to it than just their domains, however." Mr. Lorof moved to the counter near the back of the shop, where the cash register sat. Beside the register, a thick book lay open. "Professor Lasalan came to see me before she left on her research trip. She had heard rumors about elves becoming doom mages. That got me thinking and I was reading this book when those two brutes burst into my shop. If they had brains inside those skulls, they would have taken it too."

"It is known as the Staff of Skulls." Mr. Lorof lowered his voice at the mention of the name. "It is an artifact of dark intent that gave the doom mages of the past their power. The holder of the staff becomes possessed with the spirit of the Doom Master. It was destroyed in a great battle in the Dark Depths. A battle fought by the very wizards in that room. Professors Lasalan, Thornwise and Basalt all fought in the battle that destroyed the Staff of Skulls. They became known as the Heroes of the Shadow Tower."

"That explains why Professor Thornwise was so shocked to see the staff again," I said.

"I'm sure he was. Chancellor Rund, Agniz Willowseed and Inquisitor Quantz were part of the expedition into the Dark Depths too. I don't think they fought in the battle, but it was still quite an important moment in Shadow Tower history. Wizards from each of the domains had to put aside their differences to defeat the Doom Master and the Staff of Skulls." Mr. Lorof looked off into the distance, like he was reliving the memories. "Everyone thought the evil of the Staff of Skulls was gone once and for all."

"Well, it's back and creating a whole new army of doom mages," I said.

"We have to warn Chancellor Rund. She will know what to do," Mr. Lorof said.

"We already tried that," I said. "She didn't believe Aleetha and River. She was too worried about making sure the summit runs smoothly. The doom mages have some spell that distracts everybody and makes them think nothing is wrong."

"Curious," Mr. Lorof said. "Then it is up to us. We have to stop the Doom Master."

"How?" I waved my gray arms in front of the old elf's equally gray face. "We're both ghosts, remember?"

"Yes, but your friends are not." Mr. Lorof grinned. "Before I found you, I tracked down Aleetha and Tank."

"Did they see you? What did they say?"

"I did not have the strength to make myself visible to them," Mr. Lorof said. "They were hatching a plan to rescue you."

My ears perked up. "I knew they would have a plan."

"Indeed," Mr. Lorof said. "They are sneaking to the top of the Shadow Tower, searching for you. Do they realize how much danger they are putting themselves in?"

"Those are two of the bravest monsters I know," I said. "How do they know where to go?"

"The troll has a device that is guiding them."
Mr. Lorof shrugged. "I do not know what it is."

My head swam with questions. Had Tank figured out a way to track the doom mages? What was this device that was guiding them? What did they plan on doing when they found the mages? A chill ran through my ghostly body.

"They don't know about the Staff of Skulls," I said. "Those doom mages will turn Aleetha into one of them and make Tank a ghost like us."

"Worse," Mr. Lorof said. "Your friends are not prepared to face doom mages. The doom mages draw their power from the grave. They can summon things from the darkness that you do not ever wish to meet."

I gulped. "All right."

"You must find your friends and warn them to stop their rescue attempt before it's too late."

"Me? What can I do while I'm a ghost?" I said. "You'll come with me, right?"

"I cannot." Mr. Lorof sighed. "Appearing in the library and then bringing you here has worn me out. I am old. Even ghosts stuck in this realm need a rest."

"I can't do it," I said.

"You must, Fizz," Mr. Lorof said. "The Doom Master's curse will continue spreading until every wizard in the Shadow Tower is a doom mage. Slick City will be overrun."

"Slick City?" I said. "We need to warn them."

"First, you must stop your friends." Mr. Lorof stood by the front window. The light was so bright, he was hard to see. "Then tell Aleetha to warn the Merchants' Guild. They won't take too kindly to a bunch of doom mages running through their markets."

"They'll fight those skull-faced wizards?"

"Sonny, if it is to protect their business, they'll fight Firebane the dragon himself." Mr. Lorof ushered me to the door. "Now hurry. There is no time to save us."

"Save us?"

He stood at the door, nearly invisible. It wasn't the light. It was him.

"You're fading," I said.

He nodded. "As will you, if you do not hurry. We only have so much time in the ghost realm before we must either be awoken or pass on to the other side."

"I like awoken," I said.

"Then you must hurry." Mr. Lorof placed his ghostly hands on my shoulders. "I last saw your friends in the Grand Hall."

"The stairs! They're probably going up through the library."

"Be careful. It is crowded out there, and who knows how many doom mages have already been created."

"It's a good thing I'm invisible to the other wizards."

"That is partly true." Mr. Lorof frowned. "But while you walk between realms, you are still visible to the doom mages."

My tail curled. "That doesn't sound good."

Mr. Lorof shook his head sadly. "And they can do much worse than sending you to the ghost realm."

CHAPTER FOURTEEN
Ghost on the Run

Wizards ran through me.

It didn't hurt, but it sure felt weird. They hurried past on my left, on my right and straight through my ghostly body without slowing down. Being stuck in the ghost realm had its advantages. A week ago I would have avoided mages like a bonus question on a math test. Now I was diving tail-deep into a sea of spell-slingers, in search of my detective partners.

At first it was strange walking through the Mage District while it was all gray. By the time I arrived at the gates to the Bailey and the Shadow Tower, my freak-out levels had stabilized.

I had left Mr. Lorof in his bookshop. For an elf who wasn't a wizard, he sure knew a lot about magic. It must have been from reading all those books on his shelves. He was right about the regular wizards not seeing me. No one turned a head as I walked by. If I concentrated, I could make myself visible, just like Mr. Lorof had shown himself to us in the library. It wouldn't last long, and I wouldn't be able to speak, but if my plan worked it might be enough.

I moved with the crowd through the gates and to the Shadow Tower. Inside, the Grand Hall was alive with noise and magic. A band played lively music from the stage at the back of the market. A large sign announced that Chancellor Rund would be making her Wizards' Summit speech very soon. I drifted through the room, keeping an eye out for a lava elf and her very large friend. After two trips around the large room, I was still without my friends and losing hope. What if I missed them? What if Mr. Lorof was wrong about Tank's plan? I was about to give up when a flash of black hair caught my eye.

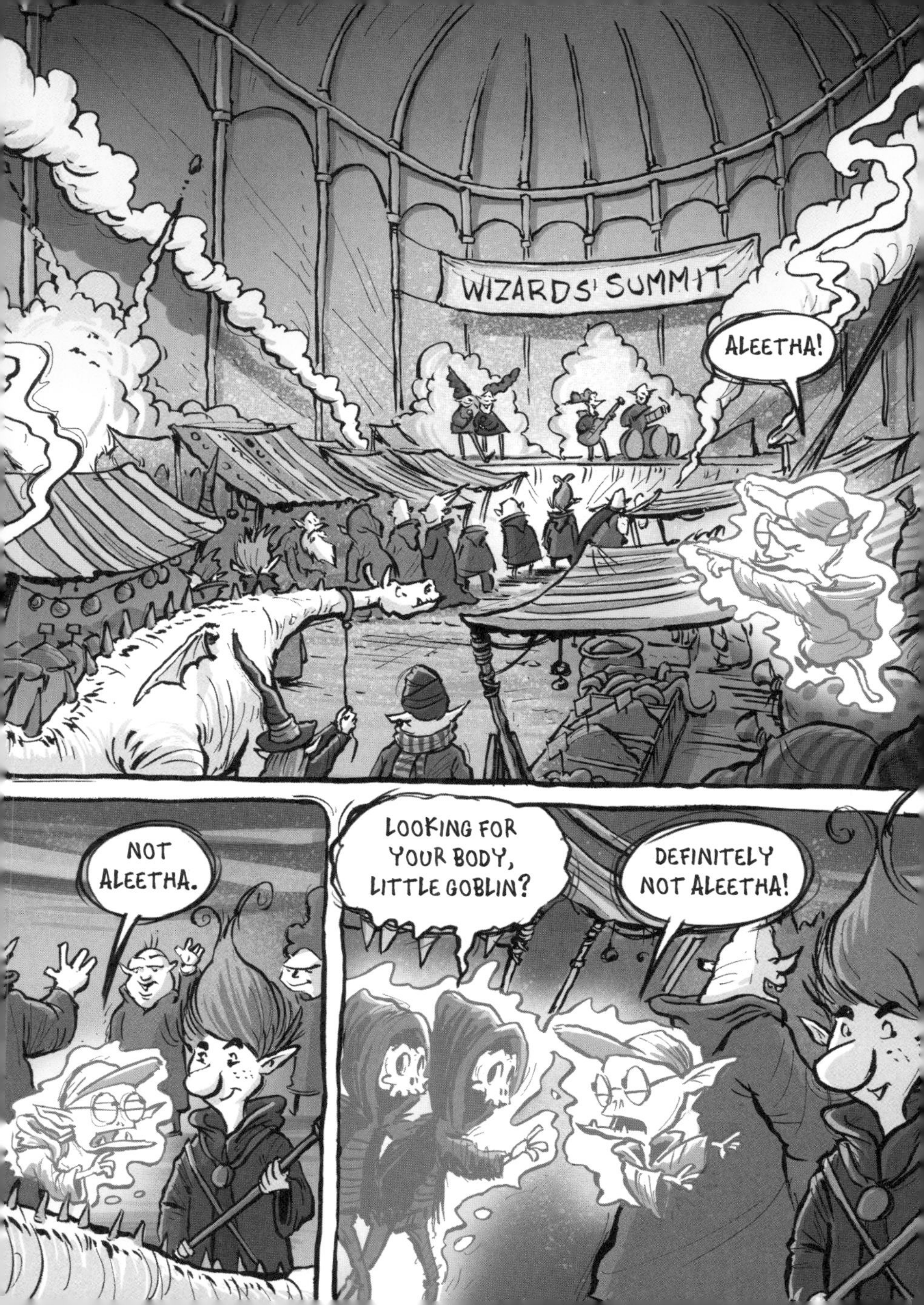
WIZARDS' SUMMIT
ALEETHA!
NOT ALEETHA.
LOOKING FOR YOUR BODY, LITTLE GOBLIN?
DEFINITELY NOT ALEETHA!

I ran, hopped and slid my way through the Grand Hall. The doom mages were on my tail every step of the way. None of the other wizards noticed a thing as the three of us raced through the room. Which was too bad, because a room full of freaking-out wizards would have been a helpful distraction at that moment. Running around the market wasn't working. I needed a new plan.

I scrambled onto the stage. The band didn't miss a beat as a ghostly goblin raced backstage. It was dark and busy with elves getting ready for the Chancellor's big speech. Even if I wasn't a ghost, I think they would have been too busy to see me sneak past them. Behind me,

I heard the doom mages jump onto the stage. In a second they would be backstage, and I'd be out of places to run. That left me with one option, an option I do very well—hide.

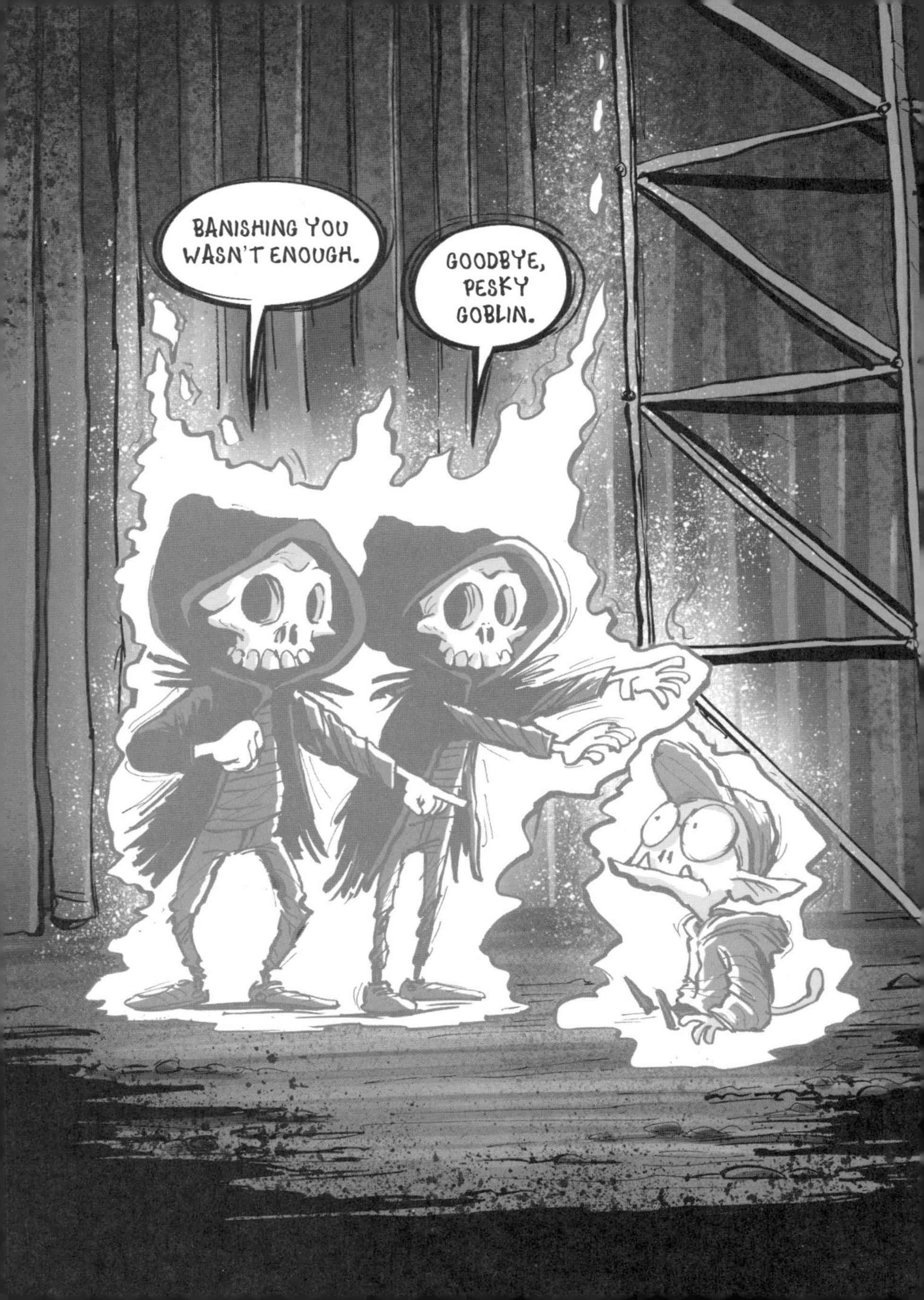
BANISHING YOU WASN'T ENOUGH.
GOODBYE, PESKY GOBLIN.

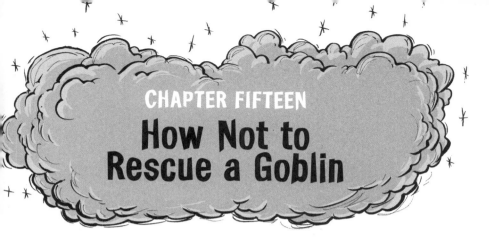

CHAPTER FIFTEEN
How Not to Rescue a Goblin

The smell of troll sweat woke me up.

The world was shaking. Three Aleethas ran behind me. I shook my head, and they blurred back into one.

"What's happening?" I croaked.

"Botched rescue mission," she said.

"Not my fault." It was a voice I'd heard since I was in diapers. "And it's not botched yet."

"Tank!"

I was slung over her shoulder like a sack of grizzlegrain, bouncing down an obsidian corridor.

"Welcome back, little buddy." Tank gave me an extra bounce and then chuckled. "Good to see you."

A deep howl sounded farther down the corridor.

"They found us," Aleetha said.

"Who found us? And how did you find me?"

"In here." Tank stopped at a tall door made of deep red clay. She tried the handle. "Locked."

Another howl came from the dark. This time closer.

Aleetha stepped to the door and hovered her hands over the carved handle. She spoke some of her magic words, and the lock tumbled. She turned the handle and pushed the door open.

"You two keep moving. I'll hold them off here."

"No way!" Tank and I said in unison.

Shapes moved in the shadows at the far end of the corridor.

Aleetha stepped into the room and Tank followed. White skulls zooming down the hall were the last thing I saw before the door closed.

Dozens of candles sparked to life as we walked in. We were in a large room dotted with wide round tables. It looked like some sort of fancy dining room. Tank moved past the tables with speed. Too much speed, actually.

"T-Tank, put me down!" I burped.

She set me down in a soft-cushioned dining chair.

I rubbed my aching tail. "What is going on? How did you find me?"

"Don't let her get to you, Fizz." Aleetha was on the far side of the room, checking the doors. She walked by a small metal serving hatch in the wall. "Tank's phone guided us to you."

Tank held up a small bottle filled with foul-smelling liquid. "And this stink juice woke you up."

"Ned got it for us." Aleetha pointed to Tank. "But twinkle-nose sneezed at the wrong moment and brought a herd of skull-faces our way."

"I think I'm allergic to magic!" Tank wailed.

A crash at the door sent it straining against its hinges.

"Okay, whatever is out there is coming in here eventually," I said.

"And we're trapped," Aleetha said. "These doors are locked."

"What about your wave-your-hands-magic stuff?" I asked.

"That's a once-a-day deal," she said. "I can only use the spells I memorize in the morning when I wake up. Once a spell is cast, I have to wait until the next day to memorize it again."

"We don't have time to wait." Tank moved behind a table. "We've got to think of something. I give that door one more hit before—"

The door exploded. Splinters of wood and wall flew at us like a swarm of dodgeballs. Sharp, pointy dodgeballs. I dove behind Tank's table and cowered. I'm good at cowering.

Dark smoke billowed into the room and gathered in a cloud at the doorway. Three snarling shapes stepped from the cloud.

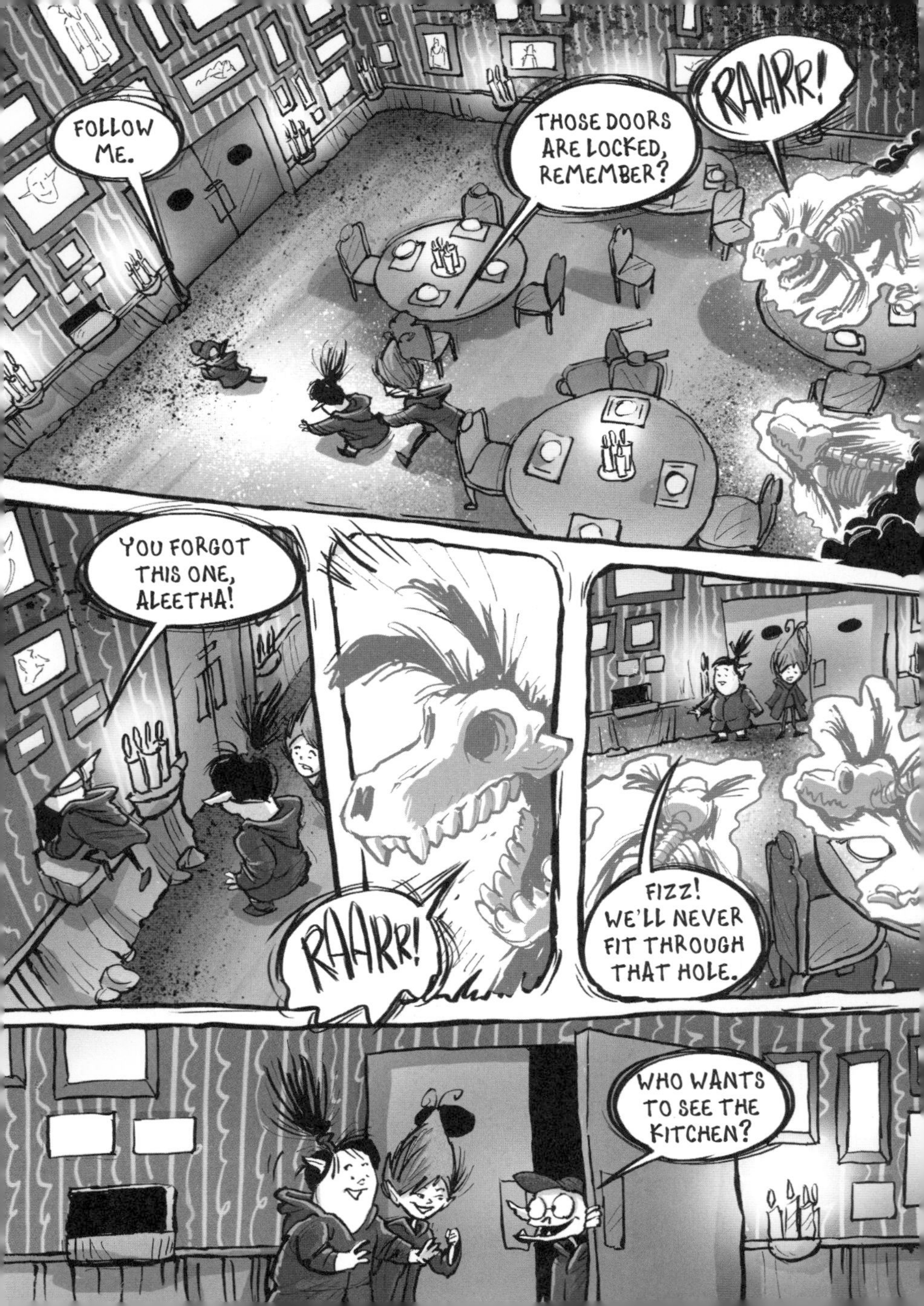
FOLLOW ME.
THOSE DOORS ARE LOCKED, REMEMBER?
RAARR!
YOU FORGOT THIS ONE, ALEETHA!
RAARR!
FIZZ! WE'LL NEVER FIT THROUGH THAT HOLE.
WHO WANTS TO SEE THE KITCHEN?

I slammed the doors shut and locked them again. Tank and Aleetha scrambled to their feet.

"Nice job, Fizz!" Tank said. "Good to have you back."

A bonehound slammed against the doors. They both buckled in the middle.

"Those won't hold for long," Aleetha said. "Keep moving."

We were at the sinks when the doors burst off their hinges. The bonehounds charged into the kitchen. Their claws scraped against the hard floor, sounding like knives being sharpened. The only exit was on the other side of the kitchen. We'd never make it. My tail drooped. My scramble through the hatch had only bought us a few seconds. It wasn't going to be enough.

"See you in ghostland," I moaned.

"Not just yet." Tank stood a few steps away, holding open a heavy metal door. Cool air billowed out the door. "In here."

"That's a walk-in fridge, Tank," I said. "We'll freeze."

"It's better than a bonehound's bite." Aleetha hurried into the fridge.

I followed her into the large fridge. Tank pulled the door shut. It closed with a satisfying thud and pitched us into darkness. Cold air filled my snout as I stood quietly, terrified to breathe too loudly.

"Bonehounds hunt by scent," Aleetha whispered. "Hopefully, the seal on that fridge door will cut off our trail."

"How did they get here?" I said. "You said you were spotted by doom mages."

"The doom mages must have summoned the dogs to do their hunting." Aleetha moved away from the door. A small ball of yellow light appeared in her hand and floated lazily into the air. The soft glow washed over the fridge, revealing rows of frozen food stacked neatly on the shelves. "I know you two like the dark, but I need some light."

We moved to the back of the fridge. Aleetha's little ball followed us and hovered just above our heads. Warmth pulsed from the ball as well as light. It helped slow the chill creeping under my scales.

"What do we do now?" I asked.

"We wait," Aleetha said. "Hopefully, those hounds will think we left the kitchen."

"Wait?" I said. "We don't have time to wait."

In a whisper, I hurriedly told them everything that had happened since I fell through the doom mage's portal.

From seeing the Doom Master transform the professors and River with the Staff of Skulls to meeting the ghost of Mr. Lorof in his shop, I spilled it all.

"Staff of Skulls?" Aleetha tapped her chin. "That is from some big battle way down in the Dark Depths. We learned about it in history class. Professor Lasalan was there. She helped destroy the staff."

"And now the staff is back somehow," I said. "All the missing mages were at the battle that destroyed the staff."

"That can't be an accident," Tank said. "The Doom Master chose those specific wizards for a reason."

Aleetha rummaged in her satchel and pulled out the Domains of Magic book.

"Maybe this will tell us." Aleetha flipped through pages. She read in whispers under the glow of her floating ball of light. "The Doom Master is not an elf or a monster. It is a creation of the Staff of Skulls itself. In its bid to survive, the staff chooses who owns it. It takes control of an unfortunate elf or monster and turns him or her into the villain that is the Doom Master."

"So the Doom Master is really one of the Shadow Tower wizards being controlled by the Staff of Skulls?" Tank scratched her ear.

"A staff that can control wizards?" I said. "I don't get it."

"Don't try. It's confusing," Aleetha said. "The thing I don't get is, what is the staff telling the Doom Master to do?"

"That part I do know," I said. "The doom mages are going to turn every wizard into one of them and then conquer Rockfall Mountain." I told them about overhearing the doom mages backstage in the Grand Hall. "They are planning to do something during Chancellor Rund's speech."

"That is happening very soon," Aleetha said. "Every wizard attending the summit will be there."

"Then we definitely do not have time to sit around. There must be another way out of here." Tank got to her feet. She moved to the back of the fridge and peered behind some boxes sitting on the frosty shelves. "Do fridges have back doors?"

"I hope so," Aleetha whispered. She stood with her ear to the fridge's front door. "I can hear those bone-hounds sniffing around out there."

"Um, guys." Tank's voice came from the shadows. "Look what I found."

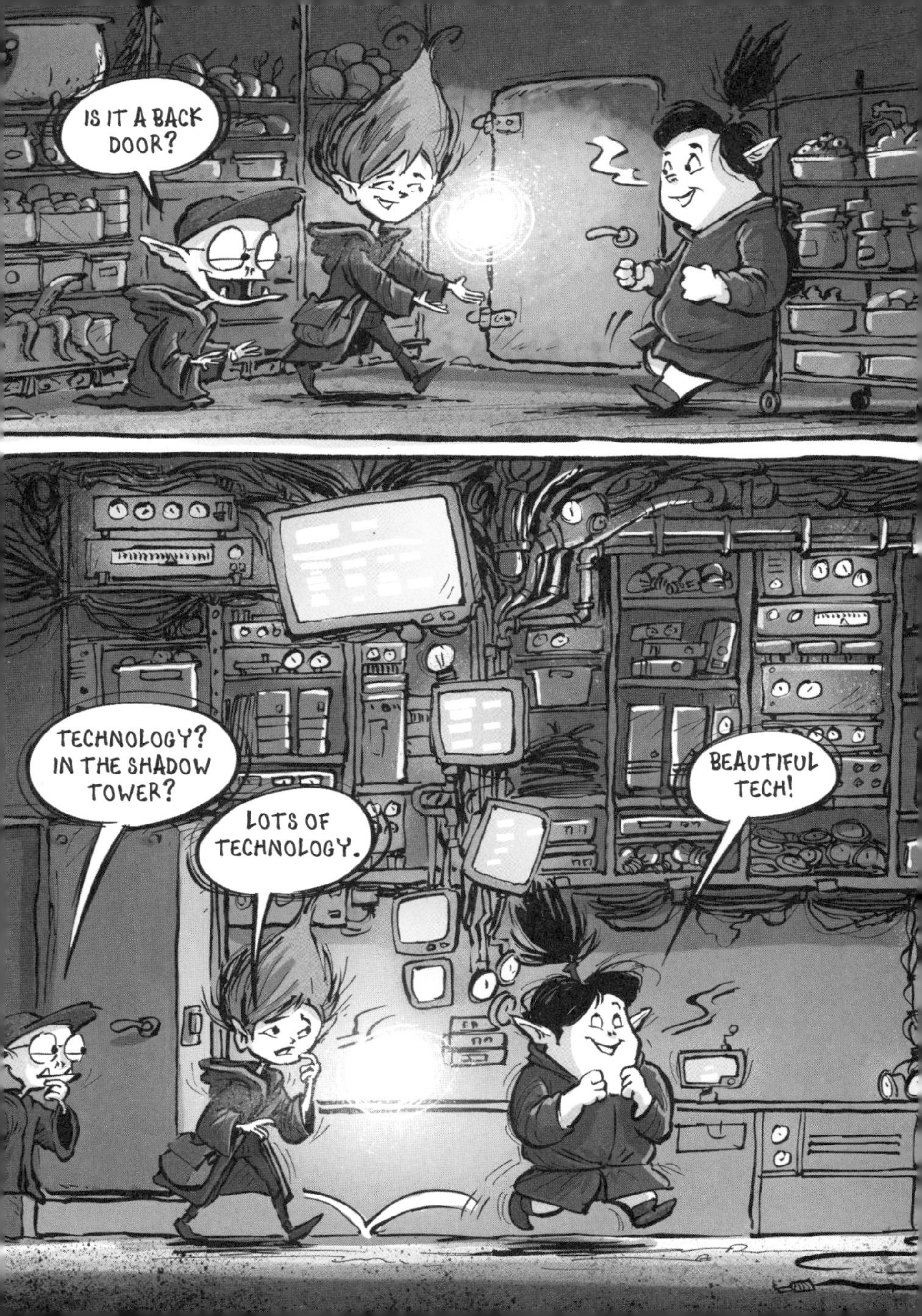
IS IT A BACK DOOR?
TECHNOLOGY? IN THE SHADOW TOWER?
LOTS OF TECHNOLOGY.
BEAUTIFUL TECH!

CHAPTER SIXTEEN

A Treasure Trove for Tank

The room in the back of the fridge was packed with technology.

Gadgets and gizmos sat neatly on shelves reaching up to the ceiling. Each piece of tech was neatly labeled and catalogued. Tank ran from shelf to shelf, touching wires and casings like she was checking to see if this was a dream.

"So much technology."

"What is it all doing here?" I said. "I thought you wizards didn't like technology."

"We don't," Aleetha said. I had never seen her look so confused. "It messes with our magic. Why is it here? Who put it here?"

"Why is it in a fridge?" I said.

"The cold air helps preserve the circuits." Tank ran her hand along the shelf, reading each label closely. "Aha! What's this? Interesting."

Tank pulled a tray from the shelf. The tray was divided into six compartments, each big enough to hold something the size of a pencil case. A small metal tube sat in five of the six compartments.

"Recognize these?" Tank grinned like it was her birthday.

"The message tube Professor Lasalan sent me!" Aleetha said.

"A Holographic Express Message Tube, to be precise," Tank said.

I pointed to the empty compartment. "One of them is missing."

Tank's ears wiggled. "Exactly."

"I don't get it," I said.

"You think Professor Lasalan came here and took that message tube?" Aleetha said.

Tank's ears doubled their wiggle speed. "I've been trying to figure out how a wizard in the Shadow Tower got a piece of technology to send out a cry for help."

"She was always fascinated by technology," Aleetha said. "She never understood why magic and tech could not get along. But she never mentioned that she had a technology collection."

"She'd probably get in a lot of trouble from the other wizards," Tank said.

"So Professor Lasalan came here when she found out the doom mages were returning." I tried to piece it all together, but one question kept nagging at me. "Why not just go to the shadow guard?"

"Maybe she did. Look what happened when we tried that." Aleetha studied the back wall of the small room like she was reading a book. "If this was Professor Lasalan's secret technology stash, then maybe it's not the only thing that's hidden here."

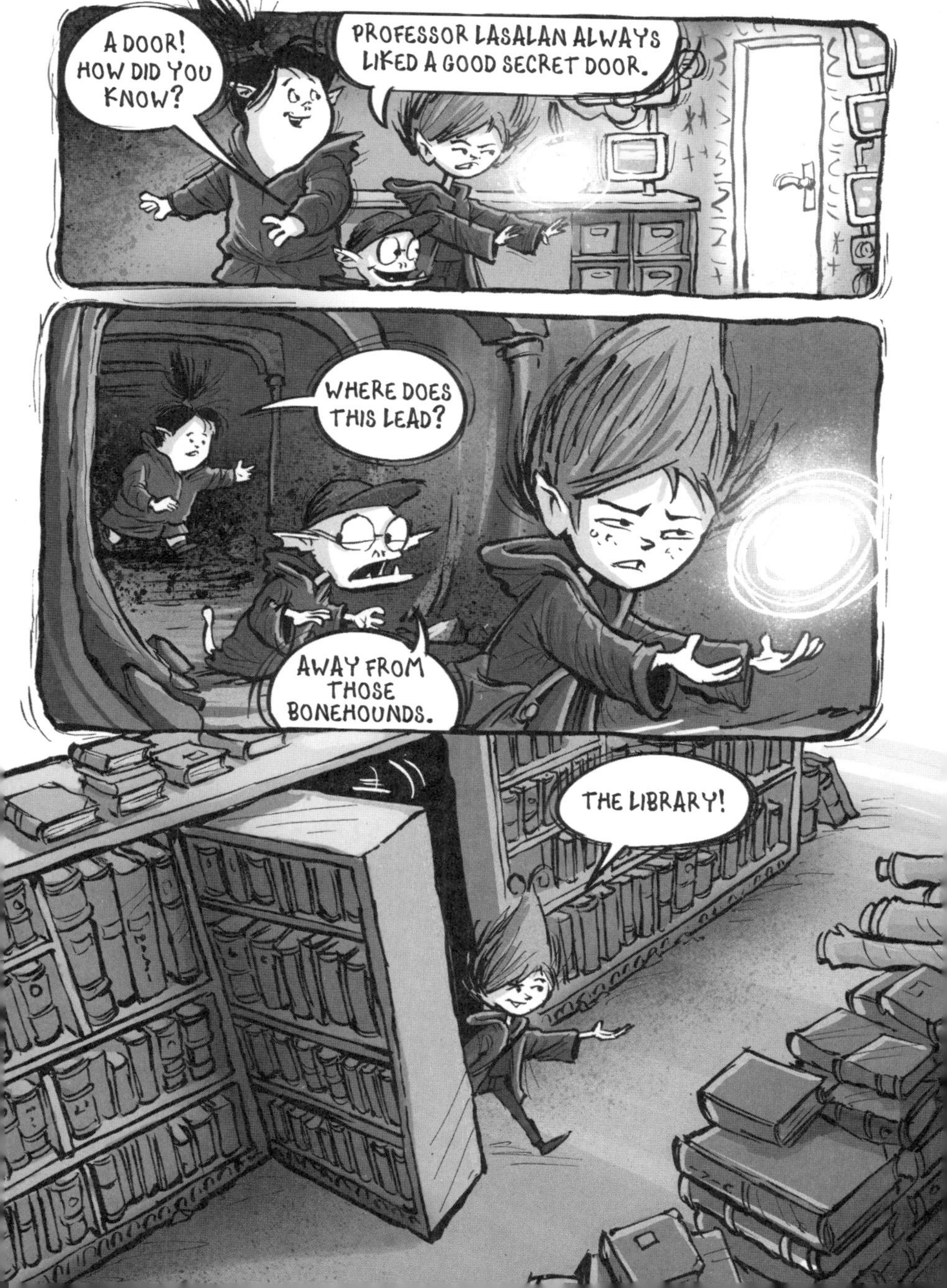
A DOOR! HOW DID YOU KNOW?
PROFESSOR LASALAN ALWAYS LIKED A GOOD SECRET DOOR.
WHERE DOES THIS LEAD?
AWAY FROM THOSE BONEHOUNDS.
THE LIBRARY!

I never thought I'd be so happy to be in a room full of books.

"That makes no sense!" Tank said. "We climbed a dozen stairs to get up to the top of the tower, and that little path brings us all the way back down here?"

Aleetha patted the troll on the arm. "Don't try to understand the Shadow Tower, Tank."

A few aisles away, books crashed to the floor, followed by a familiar shriek.

Aleetha grinned. "Excellent. Ned's here."

We followed her around the bookshelves and past the floating furniture of the air lift. I expected to see Ned the cloud elf picking himself up out of a pile of books. Instead, he was pushed against the bookshelf by an angry rock elf, and he looked terrified.

"Darnan!" Aleetha shouted. "Put Ned down."

The rock elf turned at the sound of Aleetha's voice.

"There you are!" he growled. He dropped Ned and stepped toward Aleetha. "I've been looking for you." Ned scrambled away from Darnan.

I edged closer to the air lift, ready to jump clear if the rock-head started swinging.

He wasn't in the mood to fight.

"What happened to Professor Basalt?" The anger had drained from his stony face. "You and your troll buddy show up, and he vanishes. And then you both run away. Something is going on. Tell me."

No one said anything. It was as quiet as, well, a library.

"Please?" He looked more like a sad pebble than an angry boulder.

Aleetha took a deep breath. "Darnan, if we tell you, then you've got to cut the boulder-brain bully routine. We're on the same side, okay?"

The rock elf nodded.

Aleetha shrugged. "Good enough."

"Every mage in the Shadow Tower is in grave danger."

Darnan and Ned listened as Aleetha explained what we had just discovered. She told them about the doom mages, Professor Basalt being taken and the battle for the Staff of Skulls.

Ned's eyes lit up at the mention of the battle. "We have a book on that in the history section."

The wind mage hurried along the aisle and back around the air lift without another word. We followed and found him pulling a large book from a shelf.

He carried the book to a nearby table. On the front of the book, in golden letters it read: *The Battle of Fire and Doom*.

Ned turned the pages quickly. "This is the complete story of how the Staff of Skulls was destroyed."

He stopped on a page that had a large sketch of the staff.

"That's it!" I said. "That's the staff the Doom Master used to turn your mentors into skull-faced wizards."

"Then you did see the Staff of Skulls," Aleetha said.

Ned shook his head. "That's impossible. It says here the staff was destroyed. A group of mages traveled down to the Dark Depths and ambushed the Doom Master before his army could attack."

"And now the Doom Master has ambushed them," I said. "Professors Lasalan, Basalt and Thornwise were the mages in that battle."

Tank looked at me like I had actually finished my homework for once. "How do you know that?"

"Mr. Lorof told me," I said. "He thinks the Doom Master chose those mages for a reason."

Ned scanned the page of the book. "You're right, Fizz. Basalt, Lasalan and Thornwise are all listed as fighting in the battle."

Aleetha stood next to Ned and read the page herself. "Why does it say *and others* after the list of names?"

"That I can answer," Darnan said from where he stood at the end of the table. "Professor Basalt often talked about that battle. He was quite proud of his achievements that day. Apparently, not all the mages who traveled to the Dark Depths took part in the actual fight. Only one mage from each domain could face the Doom Master."

"Of course," Ned said quickly. "Any more mages would have muddled the energy-transference rate and weakened their spells."

I looked to Tank. She shrugged. She didn't understand any of it either.

"The rest of the mages stayed out of the battle," Darnan continued. "Not all of them were happy about it. They wanted to share in the glory of defeating the Doom Master. They were not named as Heroes of the Shadow Tower but instead just received a thank-you from the chancellor of the tower."

"One of those mages is the chancellor today," I said. "Mr. Lorof told me Chancellor Rund journeyed to the Dark Depths but didn't fight in the battle. Same with Agniz Willowseed and Inquisitor Quantz."

"And now they're all here at the Shadow Tower for the Wizards' Summit," Tank said. "Interesting."

"They all helped afterward." Aleetha looked up from reading the book. "It says the Staff of Skulls shattered into small pieces before falling into the lake of lava in the Dark Depths and dissolving into ash. All the mages helped search for any remaining bits of wood. They swept them into the lava so the staff could not grow again."

"Grow again?" I said. "This staff can control an elf and turn him or her into the Doom Master and it can grow after being destroyed?"

"That's what it says here." Aleetha read from the book again. "*The Staff of Skulls can regenerate itself from the smallest splinter. Given enough time, any piece of the staff will return to its original form. It grows in the deepest darkness but withers in the loftiest light.*"

"So a small piece of the staff must have survived," Tank said.

"*It withers in the loftiest light*?" I said. "What does that mean?"

Aleetha read more of the book, then shrugged. "It doesn't say, but I know lofty means high."

"We better figure it out soon," Ned said. "Chancellor Rund's speech will be starting any minute in the Grand Hall. That's when the doom mages are going to strike."

"Has her speech already begun?" Tank checked her watch and frowned. "Why are the numbers spinning?"

"Magical particles messing with the tech. It happens." Ned shrugged. "We can watch her speech from here. We just need a float screen."

He said a few words I didn't understand. It sounded like magic to me. Then a cloud began to form in front of us. It grew quickly until it was the size of a large painting. In the center of the cloud an image appeared.

"Is that the Grand Hall?" I asked.

"It is," Ned said. "Look at those crowds. You wouldn't catch me down there. I hate crowds."

The float screen showed the Grand Hall, packed with wizards. Many of the vendors' tables had been replaced by chairs, which were filled with wizards from all magic domains. Each domain sat as a group in the audience in front of the empty stage.

Chancellor Rund came onto the stage.

"Turn up the volume," Aleetha said.

Ned waved his hand, and Chancellor Rund's voice came through the cloud.

"Thank you, everyone, for joining us for the 125th Wizards' Summit!" The crowd cheered. "We are very pleased you could be here today."

The chancellor kept talking, but I stopped listening. A group of wizards with their hoods pulled over their heads had walked onstage behind Chancellor Rund. She didn't see them and continued talking.

"Is that part of the show?" Ned asked.

Each elf was from a different magic domain. Fire, stone, air, forest and water. All domains were onstage. "Professor Lasalan!" Aleetha reached out to the float screen as if she could touch her mentor.

Tank pointed to the wood elf next to Professor Lasalan. "And that's Professor Thornwise."

The new arrivals all had one thing in common.

"They're all wearing black cloaks," I said, and I knew why. I had watched their transformation. I had seen what darkness had devoured them. "They're doom mages."

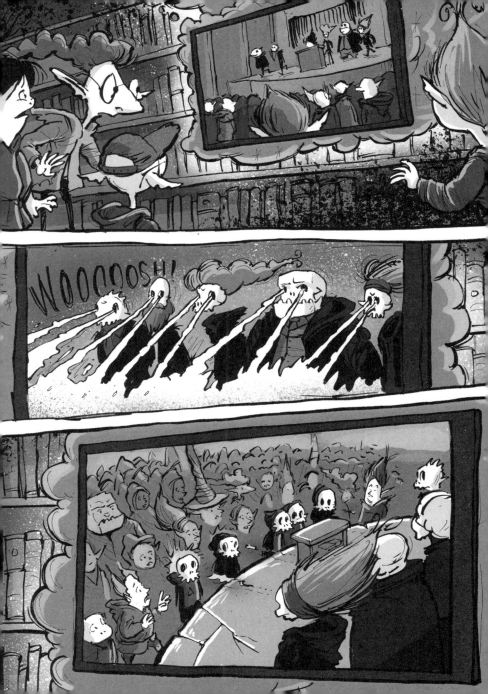

WOOOOOSH!

"They're turning the audience into doom mages!" Ned gasped.

"And all it takes is one look to transform them," Aleetha said. "We have to do something!"

"What can we do?" Ned jumped to his feet and paced back and forth. "Every wizard in the Shadow Tower is down there."

Confusion swept through the Grand Hall. On the float screen, Chancellor Rund looked into the eyes of Professor Thornwise, only to be turned into a doom mage. Behind them, another group of doom mages watched the action unfold.

"There's the Doom Master!" I said. "The one that started this whole mess." The mage held a long sinister-looking staff. Skulls floated around the top of the staff. "And that's the Staff of Skulls."

"And there's River!" Tank pointed to one of the doom mages standing beside the Doom Master. "You can tell it's her by the green things around her head. What did she call them?"

"Leaves. They're from trees that grow outside the mountain." My tail spiked to attention. My body jolted. "That's it! Leaves and trees growing!"

"What are you talking about, Fizz?" Tank said.

"The loftiest light!" I said. "The Staff of Skulls can only be destroyed by the loftiest light. That line from Ned's history book."

Aleetha recited the line from the book. "*It grows in the deepest darkness but withers in the loftiest light.*"

"River told me that trees grow from a big ball of fire high in the sky," I said.

"The sun?" Aleetha asked.

"That's it!" I said. "The sun. We have to shine the light of the sun on that staff to destroy it."

"We live under a mountain, Fizz," Ned said. "No light from outside the mountain ever shines down here."

Onscreen, wizards ran around in panic. Even the shadow guard couldn't maintain order or stop the spread of the doom mages.

"That's where you're wrong, Nedarius." I turned to Tank. "I have an idea, and I think I'm going to need some tech support from the freezer."

A grin spread across my best friend's face. "I was hoping you'd say that."

CHAPTER SEVENTEEN
Cloud-Riding Trouble

The Doom Master's chamber was as quiet as a grave. The room was empty except for the pedestal standing in the middle of the floor.

"What did they do to this place?" Darnan asked. "Last time I was up here, it was like a meeting room for the senior wizards."

"And now it's the lair of a crazed doom mage," I said.

"It's the power of the Staff of Skulls," Nedarius whispered. "Just like it can turn a wizard into a doom mage, its magic has transformed this room into an evil sanctuary."

"Just be thankful all the skull-faces are down below making other doom mages," I said.

"I'll be thankful when we've crushed the Doom Master and Professor Basalt is back," Darnan said.

I had to agree with the big rock-head. He had cooled his whole bully routine since we'd found him in the library with Ned. He'd actually offered to come up here with us, in case we ran into trouble. Which was a big change from him wanting to stuff us between the covers of the nearest book.

I slowly walked into the room, keeping my eyes on the shadows in the corner. I stopped in front of the pedestal. The Doom Master had stood here when the light of the moon fell on the Staff of Skulls and turned the professors into doom mages. A narrow shaft was carved into the ceiling directly above the pedestal. It ran straight up and disappeared into darkness. But I had a feeling I knew where it ended.

"We're on the top floor of the tower, right?" I asked when Ned joined me at the pedestal.

"Yes. The outside walls of this room connect directly with the stone ceiling of Rockfall Mountain."

From my earliest days as a little goblin, I could remember looking at the Shadow Tower and wondering what was at the very top. The dark walls of the tower stretched up into the sky over Slick City until they touched the rock that formed the room of the cavern we called home. Now I was inside the exact spot where the tower walls met the rock ceiling. And I still had farther to go.

"You sure this will work?" Ned asked. The wind mage watched the shadows. His narrow face filled with doubt.

"I haven't been sure of anything since I came here," I said. "But I'm hopeful you can help me get to where I need to go."

"I'll try." Ned stepped back. Wisps of smoke gathered around his hands. "You ready?"

"Work your magic, Nedarius."

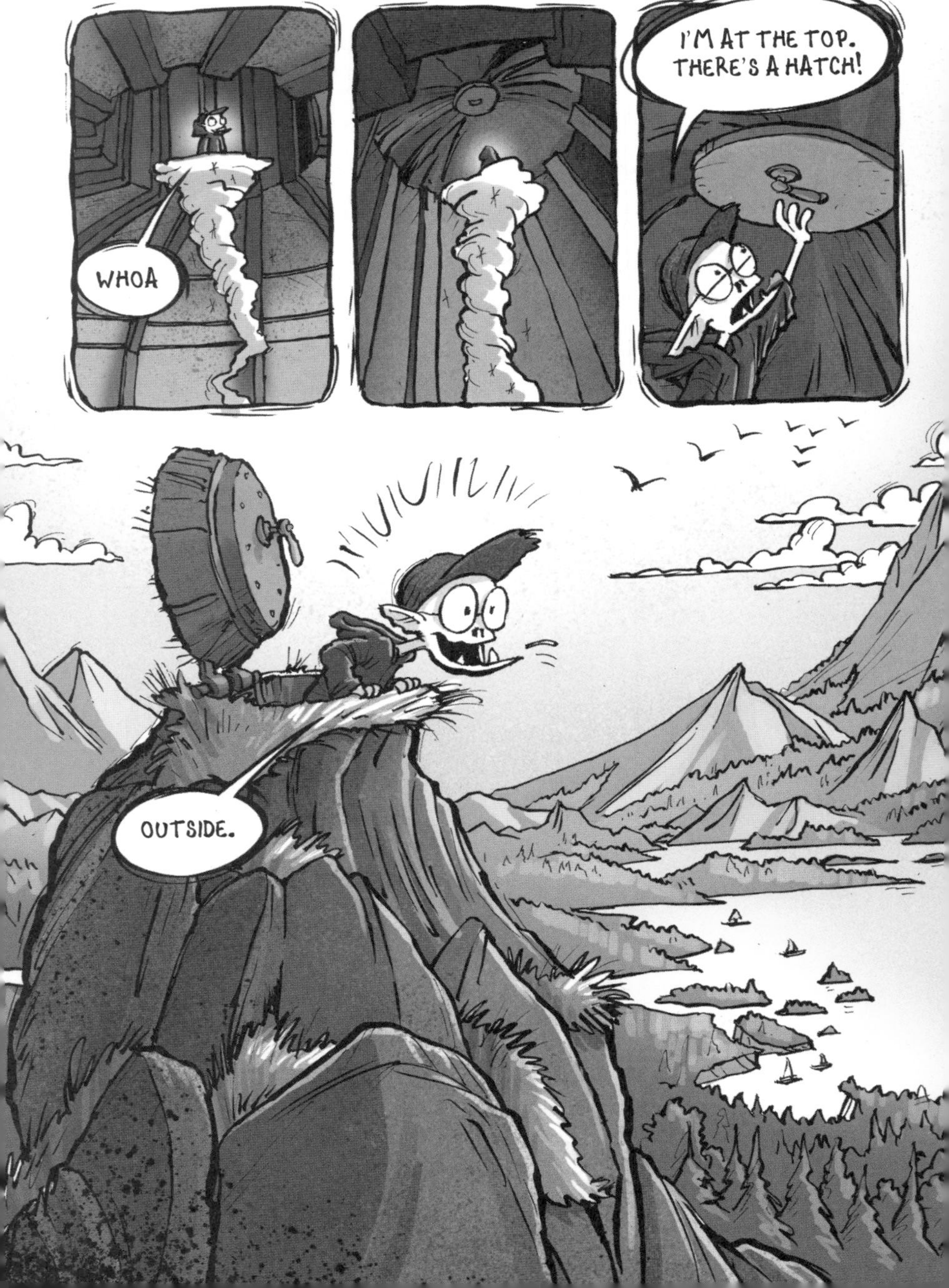
WHOA
I'M AT THE TOP. THERE'S A HATCH!
OUTSIDE.

A roof of brilliant blue spread out above my head. I had never seen so much sky before. This was way better than catching glimpses of the outside through the cave mouth in Fang Cove. The sky went on forever. Little fluffy clouds drifted slowly overhead like slow-moving ships. Below me, the jagged rocks of the mountain dug deep into the ground before ending in a blanket of green that covered everything in sight. This was outside. This was the world that River had spoken about. The world of leaves and trees, plants and animals. Hanging above all this strange wonder was the source of all life. And my only hope of saving us from darkness. I could not look at the sun for more than a moment. Its light warmed my scales, filled the shaft and pierced deep into the layers of Rockfall Mountain.

"You did it, Fizz!" Ned's words carried up to me. "It's—uh, what was that noise?"

A low growl rumbled through the chamber. Darnan shouted, and there was a crackle of magic. The cloud under my feet lurched.

A bone-white shape moved along the floor below me. I caught sight of it for only a moment, but the sound of its claws clacking on the tiled floor gripped my nerves.

Bonehounds.

Ned screamed. The cloud under my feet vanished. I fell like a stone down a well. The sunlight filling the shaft could not slow my fall or stop my panic.

The floor raced toward me in a blur. I burst from the shaft in time to see Darnan facing down a bonehound the size of a school bus. The rock elf pelted the skeleton dog with a shower of stones that did little more than annoy it. But it was enough to give Ned time to act.

The cloud elf blasted his magic at me. A new cloud appeared below me, slowing my fall and bringing me to a stop a tail's width from the ground.

"Thanks," I said when my heart started beating again.

Inside the doorway, the bonehound howled at Darnan.

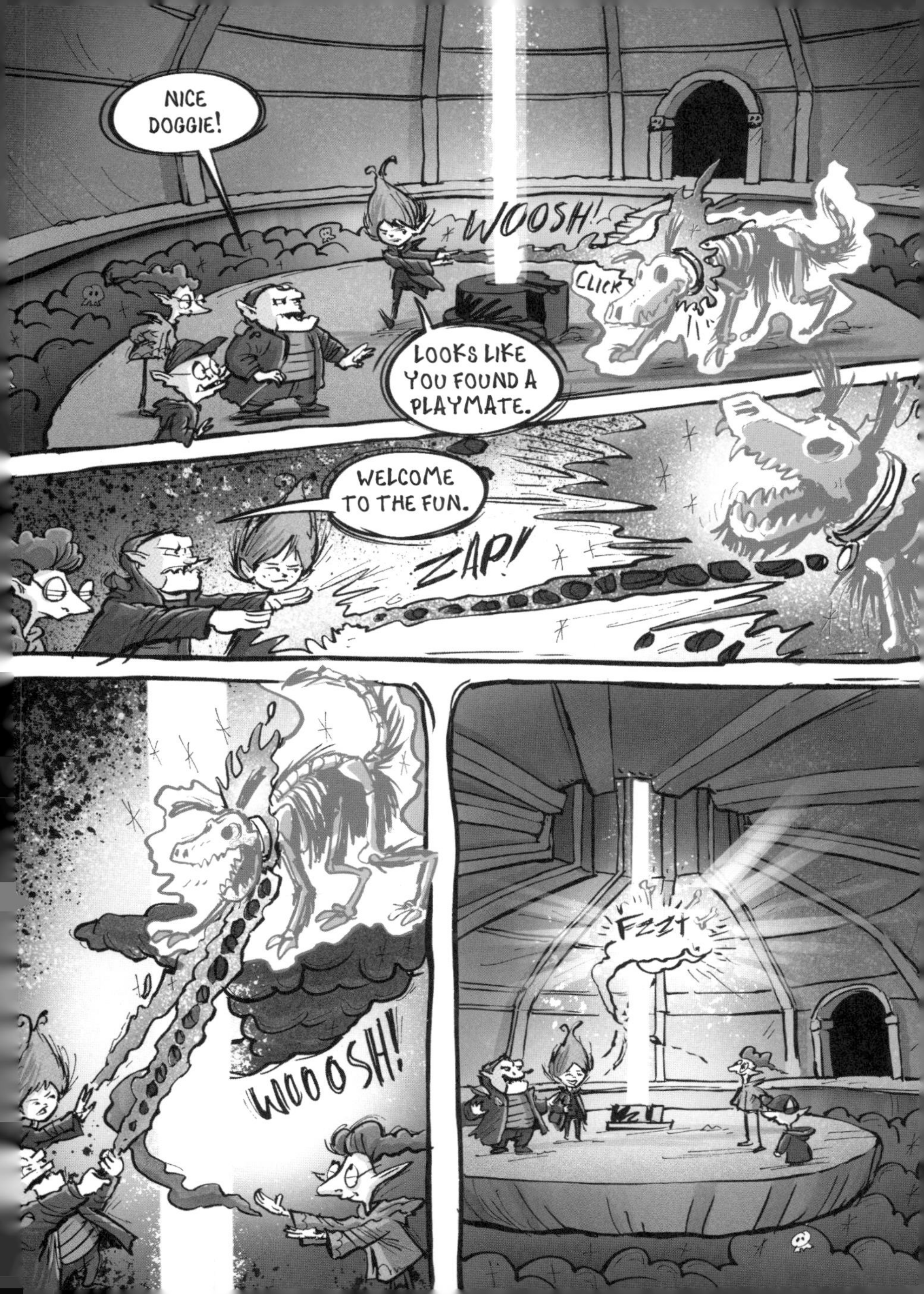
NICE DOGGIE!
WOOSH!
CLICK
LOOKS LIKE YOU FOUND A PLAYMATE.
WELCOME TO THE FUN.
ZAP!
WOOOSH!
FZZT

All that was left was a smoking pile of bones in a beautiful pool of sunlight.

I looked to Aleetha. "What are they teaching you in this school?"

"How to be a wizard." She winked. Her hands were still burning.

Tank peered around the corner. "Is it over?"

"Yes." Aleetha chuckled.

Tank looked at the pile of bones beside the pedestal. She stopped on the edge of the beam of light. Her eyes grew wide, then squinted. "If you ignore the bone-hound, it's quite beautiful. But a bit bright."

Tank saw me and smiled. She put the box on the ground.

"I brought everything we'll need." She pulled out two small metal boxes. Her ears went into wiggle overdrive. "Photovoltaic Infusion Transmitters! You can call them PITs."

"Will they do what we need them to do?" I asked.

"They're lined with energy-absorbing nanomirrors that can store and reflect particulates up to three million xenowatts."

"I think that's a yes," Aleetha said.

"They'll get sunlight into the Grand Hall?" I asked.

Tank nodded, still smiling. "I also got you this."

She pulled a small metal cylinder out of the box.

"The HEMT!" I took the message tube from her. "Excellent. Get the temporal whatever-it's-called into position. I'm going to call for backup."

I turned on the HEMT and left a rushed message. I had no idea if any of this plan would work. This message was the least I could do. I told the message tube where to go. It beeped with satisfaction and disassembled itself into a countless number of bits. In about one minute, it would reassemble itself at its destination and deliver the message.

I hurried back to the others.

"Okay," I said. "Now for part two of the plan."

"We have a part two?" Tank asked. She didn't look up from adjusting a notched dial on one of the PITs.

"Yes," I said. "Ned and Darnan are going to wake Mr. Lorof, remember?"

Ned pulled out a small vial of yellow liquid. "This will snap him out of whatever spell put him into the ghost realm."

It was the same stuff Aleetha had used to wake me from the ghost realm. I hoped it would work on Mr. Lorof too. My tail tingled. An idea took shape.

"Does it have pepper granite?" I asked.

"A whole bunch," Ned said.

"You have another vial?"

He reached into his robes and pulled out an identical vial of yellow liquid. He handed it to me.

"Be careful. It's pretty stinky. One whiff of this stuff is enough to snap anyone out of a magical enchantment."

"Perfect." I took the vial and slipped it into my pocket. "Mr. Lorof is on this floor somewhere. Bring him to the front gates of the wall as soon as you can. If my message arrives, the reinforcements will be there."

Ned and Darnan ran out of the room. Tank gave the PITs a final adjustment, stood up and stretched.

"That should do it." She put something flashing and sharp in her tool belt. She gave me one of the PITs and held the other. "Stand there and don't do anything."

"Sure, give me the hard job."

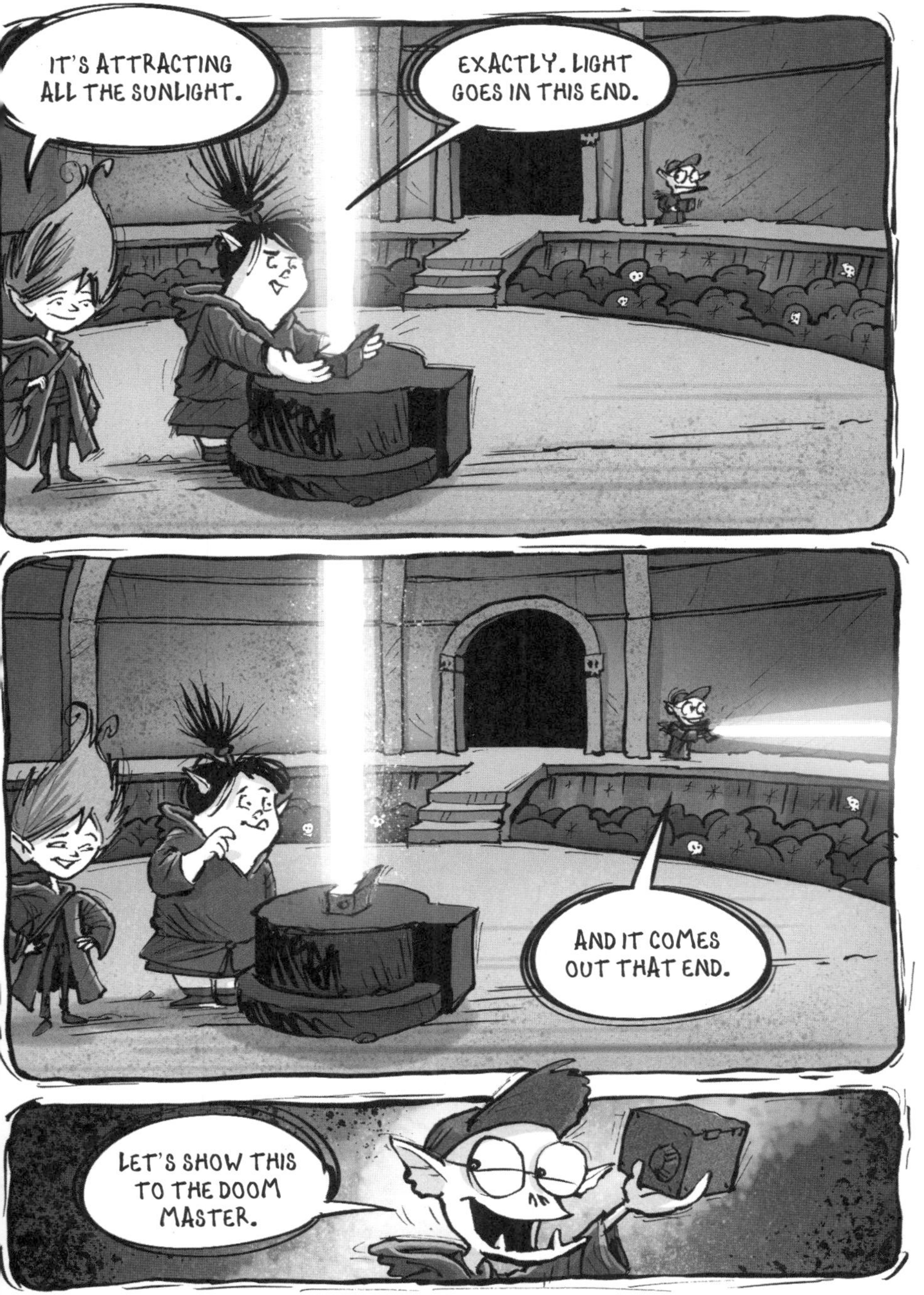
IT'S ATTRACTING ALL THE SUNLIGHT.
EXACTLY. LIGHT GOES IN THIS END.
AND IT COMES OUT THAT END.
LET'S SHOW THIS TO THE DOOM MASTER.

CHAPTER EIGHTEEN
Doom Mage Disaster

The Grand Hall was a wizard war zone.

Chairs lay scattered, bent and broken across the hall. Standing on broken glass in many perfectly straight lines was an army of doom mages. Every wizard in the Grand Hall had been transformed. It looked like there had been a struggle, but in the end the doom mages had won.

"This is bad," Aleetha said from the bottom of the stairs.

Tank scratched her ear. "What are they doing?"

"I have no idea," Aleetha said.

As a group, the doom mages faced one figure on the stage at the front. Short, round and totally evil.

"The Doom Master!" I hissed.

"Rise, Doom Mages of the Shadow Tower!" the Doom Master bellowed to the crowd of skull-faces. "Today we march beyond these walls. Today we regain the power taken from us by a band of fools who fancied themselves heroes." Onstage, five doom mages with big collars stepped forward. "Those fools are now my generals."

"Professor Lasalan!" Aleetha whispered.

Aleetha's mentor stood on the stage, next to Professor Thornwise and the other missing mages. Their faces were still skulls, their minds still under the command of the Doom Master.

The Doom Master continued to rally the army of black-cloaked mages.

"We will pour forth from the gates of the Shadow Tower and swarm Slick City." The Doom Master slammed the massive Staff of Skulls into the stage. It lit the stage with its ring of floating skulls at the top and gnarly end. The thud echoed throughout the hall.

I jumped. And I remembered something. I had heard that staff before. I reached into my pocket and felt the vial of yellow liquid.

The Staff of Skulls pulsed with a ghostly light that

drained my will just looking at it. The Doom Master pointed the staff at the back of the Grand Hall.

"Mages of the darkness! Behold my power!"

A ball of pale brightness burst from the Staff of Skulls and soared over the heads of the doom mages. As it flew, the ball of light was transformed into a skull with wild and empty eyes. Its cackling laughter echoed throughout the hall and froze my scales. In a flash, the skull crashed into the back wall of the Grand Hall with a blast that sent bricks flying.

When the smoke cleared, the wall of the Grand Hall was gone. A clear path to the Bailey and the main gates lay before the army of doom.

"Onward!" thundered the Doom Master. "Do not stop until Slick City has fallen."

A beast-like roar rose up from the gathered mages. They charged out of the destroyed Grand Hall and into the Bailey. The Doom Master's battle had begun.

"We're too late." Tank slumped against the wall. "We'll never get close enough to the staff to blast it with sunlight."

I pushed away the growing dread that my friend was right. We were running out of time. If the doom mages made it beyond the walls around the Shadow Tower, my hometown would be skull-face central. A swarm of doom mages raced by the doorway on their way out of the Grand Hall. My brilliant plan to stop the Doom Master now seemed futile. We were trapped. One look at Aleetha and the skull-faces would turn her into a doom mage too, just like they had River. If Tank and I were spotted, it would be a one-way ticket to the ghost realm.

Aleetha pulled us back from the doorway.

"There's enough doom and gloom out there without you two adding more." She adjusted her wizard's cloak and fixed us both with her fiery gaze. "We are the only ones who know what's going on. And we're the only ones who can stop it. So quit moping and follow me. I know another way out."

She didn't wait for us to answer. She turned and hurried down a narrow corridor running off from the foot of the stairs. We followed her along the twisting hallway, which ended in a small door.

"This door leads to the Bailey," Aleetha said. "Ready?"

I gulped. "Can we say no?"

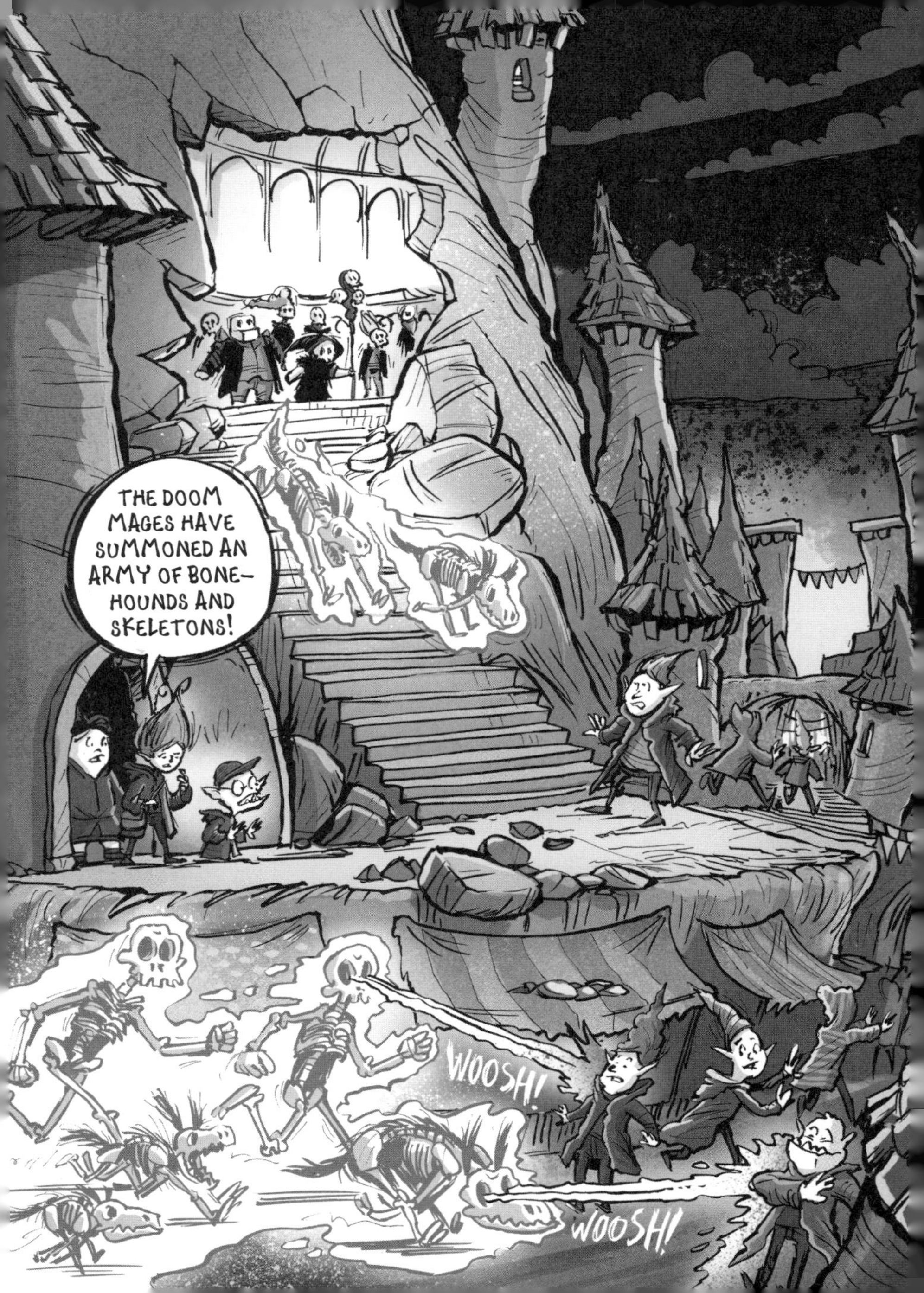
THE DOOM MAGES HAVE SUMMONED AN ARMY OF BONE-HOUNDS AND SKELETONS!
WOOSH!
WOOSH!

The Bailey was a blur of skulls, bones and chaos. Doom mages chased down the last few remaining wizards. They summoned deadly beasts of darkness to hunt fleeing merchants, sending them to the ghost realm with one bite. A few brave wizards and merchants tried to fight back, but hope of victory dwindled with every skull blast.

The Doom Master watched the battle from the top of the stairs leading into the destroyed Grand Hall. Surrounded by the professors-turned-generals, the Doom Master fired a barrage of blasts from the Staff of Skulls into the crowd. The flying skulls cackled as they smashed into wizards and turned them into doom mages. It would not be long before the Doom Master's army was ready to march on Slick City. If we wanted to stop the army, we had to deal with its master.

Tank looked at the PIT device she had given me. "You sure you want to do this?"

"No," I said. "But we agreed. I'm the smallest."

"And the slipperiest." Aleetha punched my shoulder gently. "We'll get you close enough to the Doom Master."

"Just turn that handle and it will pop open." Tank pointed to the small handle on the box's lid.

"And you're sure the sunlight will shoot out?" I asked. We had gone over this upstairs, but after all we'd been through, I was just happy I remembered my name.

Tank nodded. "Point it at that staff and hope your idea works."

We headed into the battle with our hoods pulled over our heads. By moving fast, avoiding eye contact with doom mages and sticking together, the three of us made it to the foot of the stairs. We were steps away from zapping the Staff of Skulls with sunlight when disaster struck.

A ghostly skull careened down from above and slammed into the ground in front of us. The blast of doom energy sent me flying. My scales crunched as I landed near the top of the stairs. Tank and Aleetha were gone. I frantically scanned the mass of mages for my friends, but there was no sign of them. The explosion must have knocked them into the crowd of wizards. They were gone, but I was far from alone.

The Doom Master stood steps away, surrounded by the skull-faced generals. Professors Thornwise, Lasalan and Basalt hurled skulls down on the last few wizards not yet under their master's spell.

I gripped the PIT device tightly and scrambled to my feet. The Doom Master sensed my movement and looked my way.

"Fizz Marlow. You are a persistent little goblin, aren't you?"

The dead eyes of the Doom Master burned into me. Fear gripped my scales. I fumbled with the handle of the PIT, but my fingers refused to work. Thankfully, my voice did.

"You are not the Doom Master," I croaked. "You are Agniz Willowseed!"

The Doom Master pounded the Staff of Skulls into the ground, just as Agniz had done during her presentation only hours before. The ground shook, but I stayed standing.

"The Staff of Skulls has possessed you, Agniz!" I said. My fingers continued to struggle with the handle while my brain struggled to buy time. "You were angry that you were not allowed to join the battle in the Dark Depths to destroy the Staff of Skulls. Professor Thornwise and the others only let you clean up after the battle. But you didn't sweep all the splinters into the lava, did you? You took a piece of the staff for yourself and kept it hidden. It was your little secret."

"Lies," the Doom Master growled, but she did not blast me back to the ghost realm.

A spark flashed in those dead eyes. Under that skull face, a struggle had begun. An elf who had been held captive as much as any other wizard in the tower was waking. Agniz was fighting back.

The handle on the PIT finally clicked, but I did not open it. Perhaps there was another way to save the old wood elf.

"The splinter began to grow," I said. "It spoke to you, filling your mind with thoughts of revenge. You nurtured it as it grew in darkness. All those years, the staff corrupted you and turned you into the Doom Master. But you are Agniz Willowseed. Put down the staff and be free from the Doom Master."

Around me, the battle for the Bailey was nearly complete. The gates would open soon. The horde of doom mages and their skeleton beasts would descend on my hometown.

A low rumble came from the Doom Master. It took me a second to realize the sound was laughter.

"You are a fool, Fizz Marlow," the Doom Master said. The spark was gone. The dead eyes had returned. "Agniz Willowseed is no more. Just as you will be nothing but a memory when your friend is finished with you."

The PIT device crashed to the ground behind Professor Basalt and out of reach.

"What's the matter, goblin? Lost your toy?" The rock elf grabbed at me with his large boulder hand.

I scrambled back, dodging the doom mage's stony snatch by a tail's width. I jumped to my feet, panic charging through me. I had to get to the PIT device and get that sunlight pointed at the Staff of Skulls.

Professors Thornwise and Lasalan stepped away from the Doom Master's side and turned their bony gaze on me.

"What have we here?" Professor Lasalan snarled.

"The goblin must be banished," Professor Thornwise growled.

I stumbled back as the three doom mages closed in. Behind them, the gates out of the Shadow Tower wall swung open. The army of bonehounds stormed out of the gates and charged toward Slick City.

"Onward, my beautiful creatures of doom!" the Doom Master bellowed.

My strength drained from me. It was all over. My city was doomed. We had lost.

I braced myself for the final blow from the skull-faced professors. I was going back to the ghost realm. And this time I wasn't coming back.

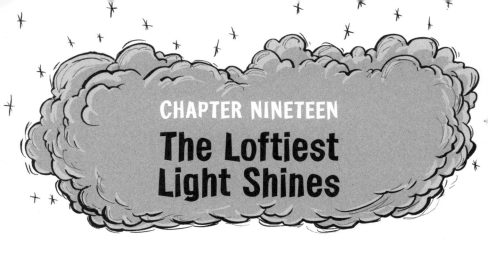

CHAPTER NINETEEN
The Loftiest Light Shines

The stinky stuff started to work.

Through the legs of the Doom Master and the professors, River began to move. Ned wasn't joking about the power of that stuff. My splash had knocked her flat. Didn't seem to do much to the professors. They were still skull-faced and looming.

River was a different story. Whatever was in Ned's potion was strong enough to snap the wood elf out of the Doom Master's enchantment.

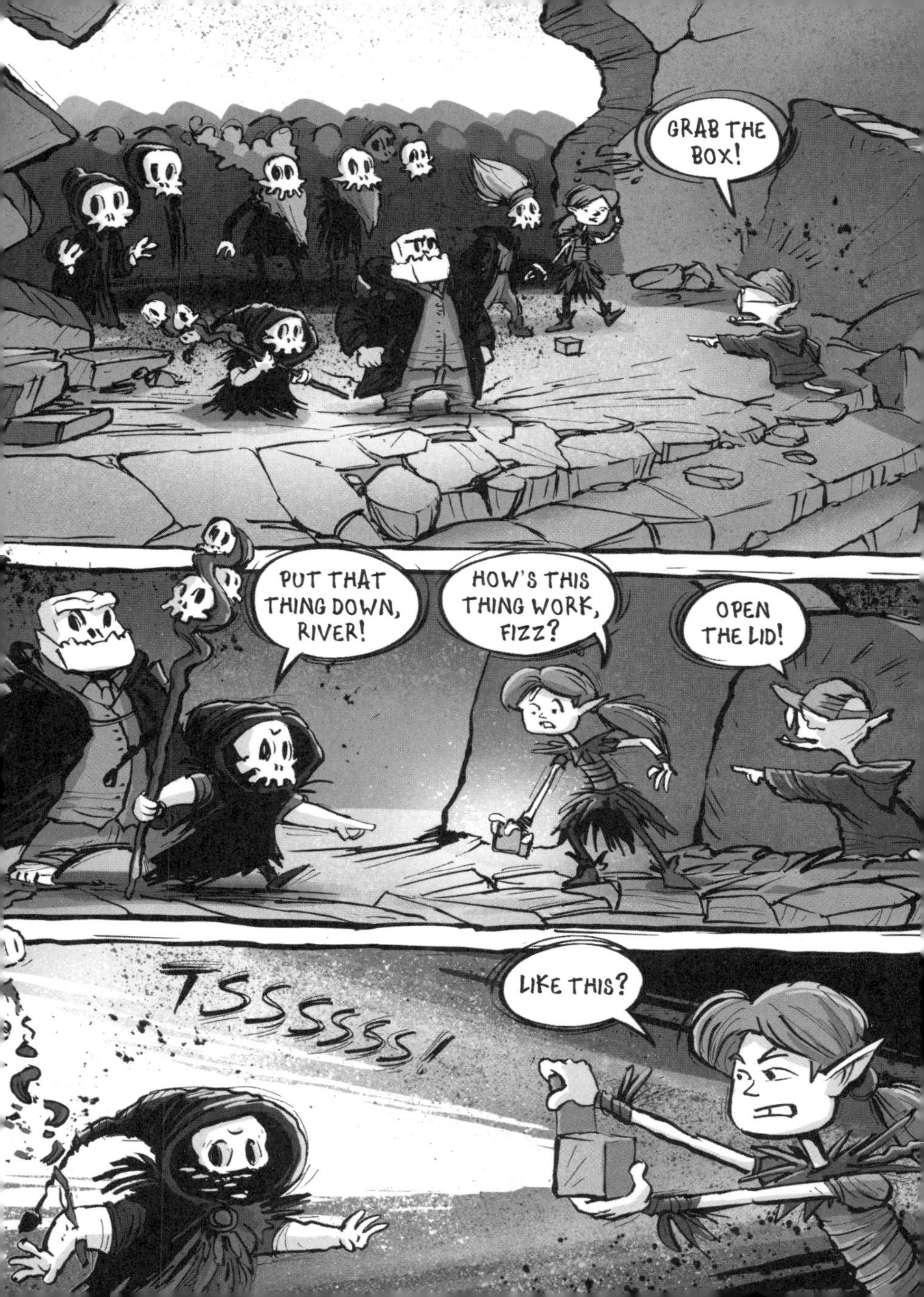
GRAB THE BOX!
PUT THAT THING DOWN, RIVER!
HOW'S THIS THING WORK, FIZZ?
OPEN THE LID!
TSSSSSSS!
LIKE THIS?

The flames devoured the Staff of Skulls, turning the cursed wood to ashes. As the staff burned, its dark magic unraveled. Across the Bailey, skull-faced wizards transformed back into elves.

With the staff destroyed, its power vanished. The Doom Master's skull disappeared, revealing the grandmotherly face of Agniz Willowseed, the source of all the chaos.

She looked at the destruction around her. "What have I done?"

"It wasn't you, Professor," I said. "You were under the control of the Staff of Skulls. It's over now."

River stepped closer and paused. Then she hugged her mentor. "Oh, Agniz. I'm so glad you're back."

Inquisitor Quantz hurried up the steps to the Grand Hall with two shadow guards at his side. The guards moved to either side of Agniz.

"You will have to come with us, Professor," Quantz said.

Professor Willowseed allowed the guards to lead her into the Shadow Tower.

"What will happen to her?" River asked.

"She will face the Council. They will decide what is to be done." Quantz turned to River and me. His eyes narrowed as he took in my non-elfish features. "Although I'm not pleased to see a goblin beyond the gates, the Shadow Tower owes you both thanks."

"And so do we." Professor Lasalan stood with Professors Thornwise and Basalt. The lava elf took in my gobliny good looks with a grin. "You must be Fizz. Aleetha has told me much about you. Where is she and your friend Tank?"

My scales spiked. Tank and Aleetha! What happened to them? Where did they go?

"Calm yourself, Fizz Marlow," Quantz said. "Your friends are at the front gates, helping Chancellor Rund clean up. They snuck through the gates in the chaos. They are looking for you."

I ran with River through the front gates of the Shadow Tower, my wizard's hood down and my goblin tail swinging free. The time for disguises was over. But as I ran through the gate in search of my friends, it looked like the battle was still going on.

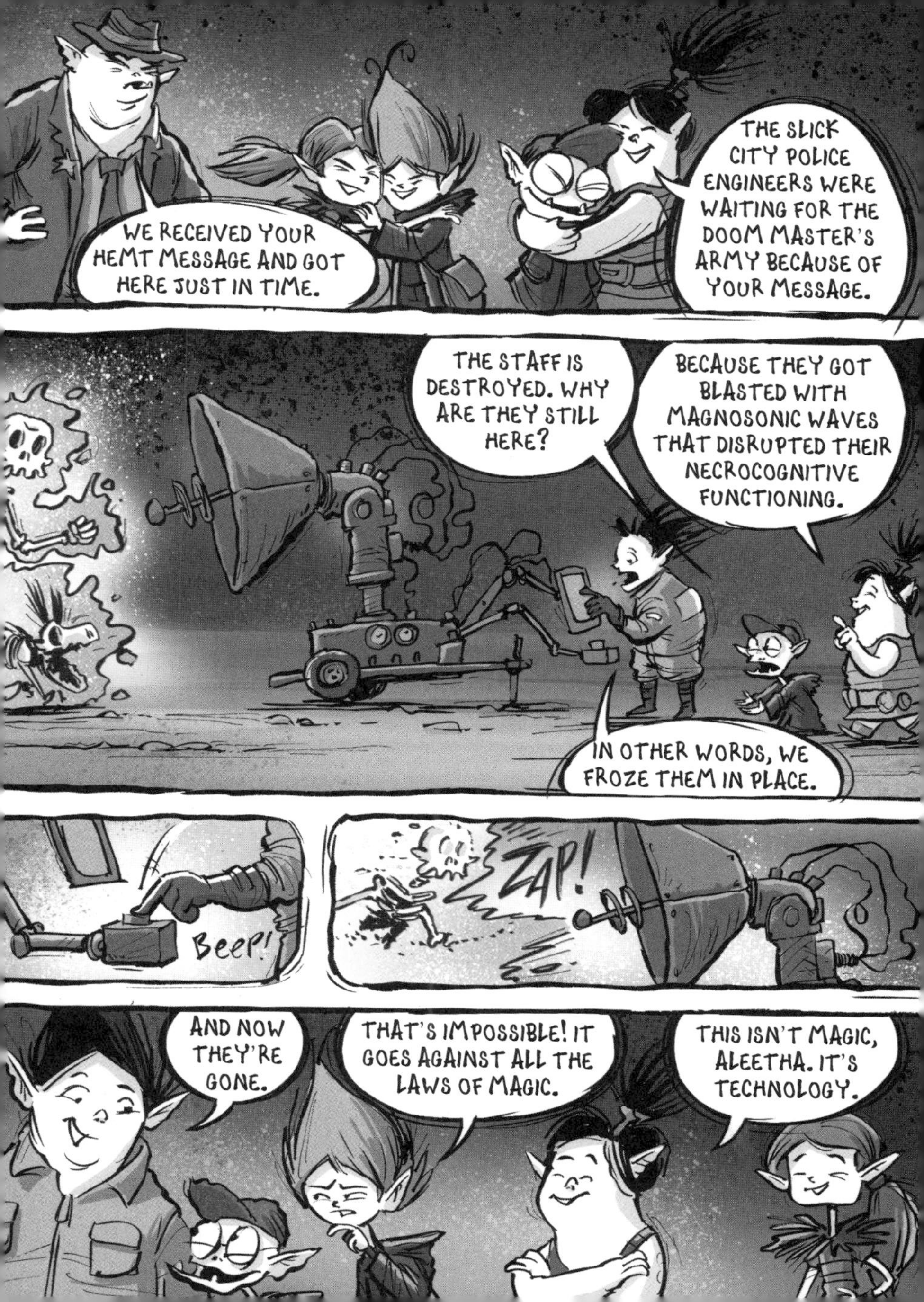
WE RECEIVED YOUR HEMT MESSAGE AND GOT HERE JUST IN TIME.
THE SLICK CITY POLICE ENGINEERS WERE WAITING FOR THE DOOM MASTER'S ARMY BECAUSE OF YOUR MESSAGE.
THE STAFF IS DESTROYED. WHY ARE THEY STILL HERE?
BECAUSE THEY GOT BLASTED WITH MAGNOSONIC WAVES THAT DISRUPTED THEIR NECROCOGNITIVE FUNCTIONING.
IN OTHER WORDS, WE FROZE THEM IN PLACE.
BEEP!
ZAP!
AND NOW THEY'RE GONE.
THAT'S IMPOSSIBLE! IT GOES AGAINST ALL THE LAWS OF MAGIC.
THIS ISN'T MAGIC, ALEETHA. IT'S TECHNOLOGY.

Fire burned in Aleetha's hands. I stepped in between my two best friends before we had a troll fire on our hands.

"Let's not restart the technology-versus-magic battle again," I said. "We just stopped a major war. Besides, Aleetha, there's someone who wants to see you."

Coming through the Shadow Tower gates was the wizard who had started us on this case.

"Professor Lasalan!" Aleetha ran to the gates and threw her arms around her mentor. "You're back!"

"Thanks to you and your friends, we're all back," Professor Lasalan said. "I knew I could count on you, Aleetha."

Behind Professor Lasalan, Professors Thornwise and Basalt came through the gates. They both still looked confused about their recent transformations from the Doom Master's generals. Alongside them stood Nedarius, Darnan and Mr. Lorof.

The old bookseller cheered when he saw me. "You did it, sonny! You destroyed the Staff of Skulls."

"River did the hard part. I just got knocked around a bit," I said. "I'm glad to see you made it out of the ghost realm."

"Thank you for sending your friends to find me." Mr. Lorof tousled Ned's hair. "But I'm never drinking that yellow gunk again!"

"I said I was sorry about that!" Ned said with a laugh.

That got me laughing. Tank started to chuckle, and then Aleetha snickered. Soon we were all giggling like a bunch of toddlers at a ticklefest. Blame it on exhaustion, too many hits to the scales or that we were all still in one piece. A good laugh was just what we needed.

Behind us, the repairs to the Shadow Tower had already begun. Boulder mages harnessed ancient spells to rebuild the stones of the Grand Hall. In front of the gates, Detective Hordish and Slick City's finest were packing up their gear and getting ready to leave.

The city and the tower were safe. Tech-crunching monsters and spell-slinging elves had worked together to save the day. I guess it didn't really matter if you had fur or scales or used wrenches or wands. For all of us, this big mountain was our home.

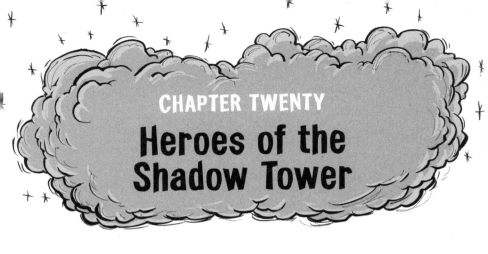

CHAPTER TWENTY
Heroes of the Shadow Tower

A week later, the Grand Hall was packed with more than just wizards.

Elves of all shapes and sizes packed into the newly and magically repaired Shadow Tower and sat alongside a handful of goblins, trolls and ogres. It was a first in the history of the Shadow Tower. A ceremony was about to begin, and Tank and I were the guests of honor.

"I can't believe Chancellor Rund let my mom and sisters into the Shadow Tower." Tank pointed out Dreena and Draana to me in the crowd. Her sisters weren't hard to miss. They were the ones bouncing liked zipped-up mudballs. Tank's mom tried to settle them down, with little success. "Your mom looks proud, Fizz."

My mom sat with Tank's mom and helped her corral the twins.

"She invited every relative over," I said with dread. "They're waiting for us back home."

Tank wiggled her ears at me. "Hope your cute little cheek scales are ready for some squeezing."

Aleetha ran across the foyer toward us.

"Darnan, River and Ned have already left!" she said, out of breath. "We've got to go!"

We ran into position just as the curtain in front of us lifted.

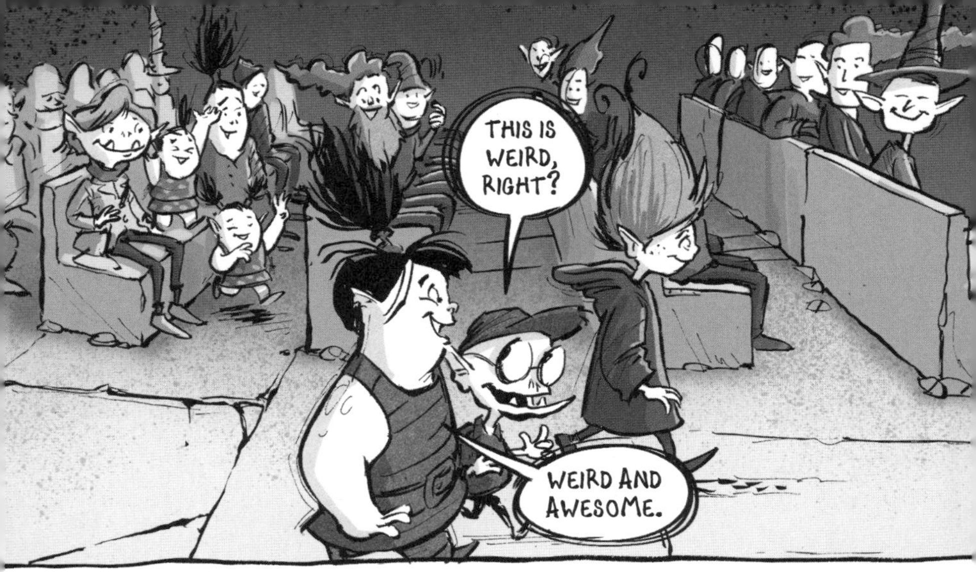
THIS IS WEIRD, RIGHT?
WEIRD AND AWESOME.

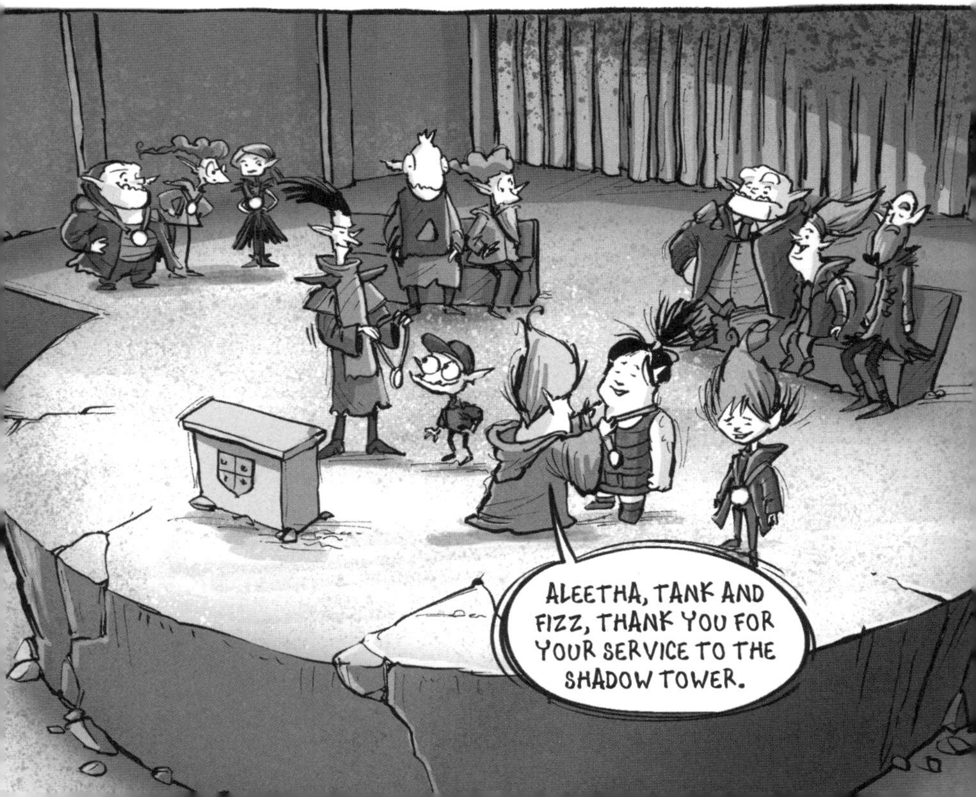
ALEETHA, TANK AND FIZZ, THANK YOU FOR YOUR SERVICE TO THE SHADOW TOWER.

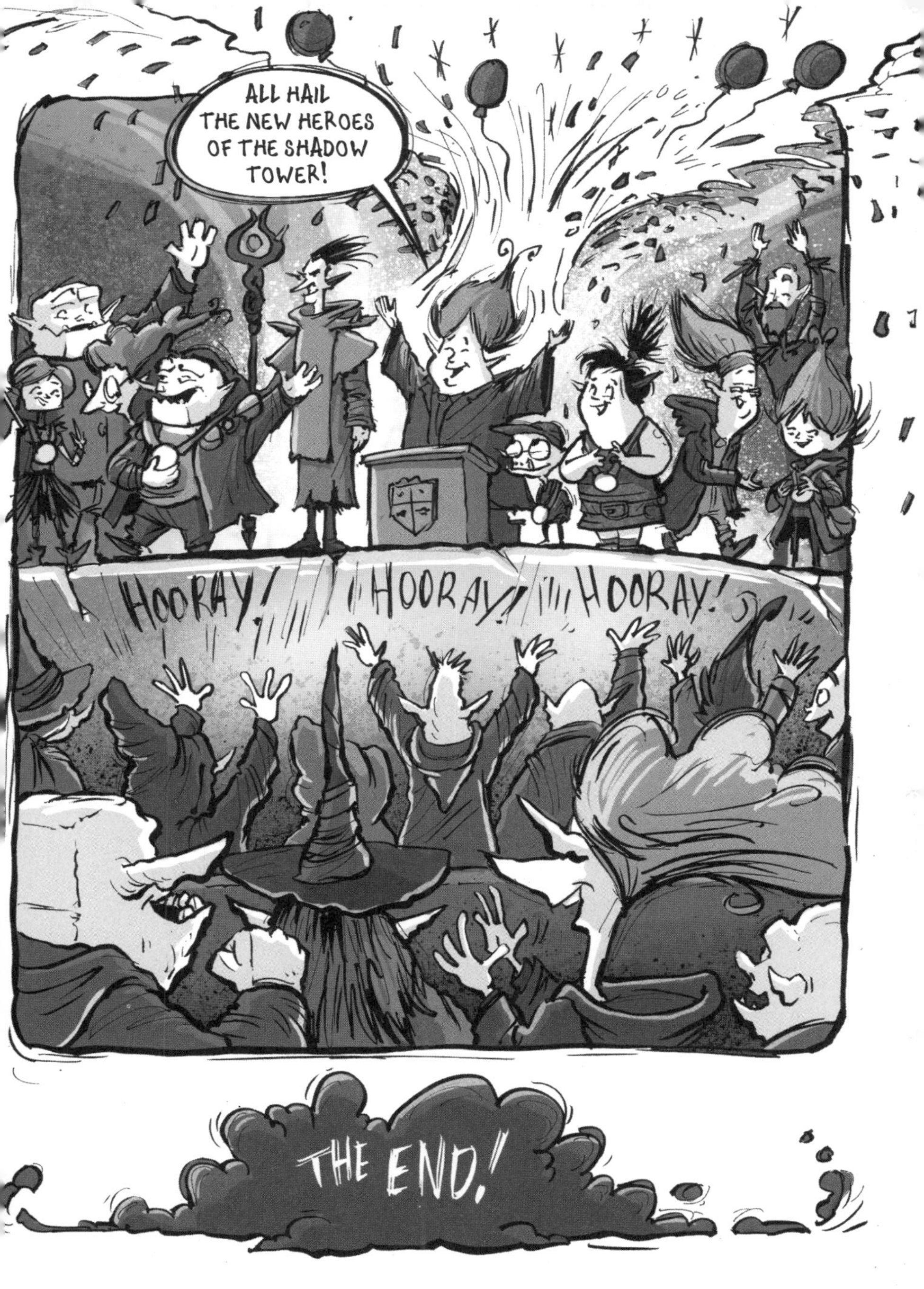
ALL HAIL THE NEW HEROES OF THE SHADOW TOWER!
HOORAY! HOORAY! HOORAY!
THE END!

LIAM O'DONNELL is an award-winning children's book author and educator. He's written over thirty-five books for young readers, including the *Max Finder Mystery* and *Graphic Guide Adventure* series of graphic novels. Liam lives in Toronto, Ontario, where he divides his time between the computer and the coffeemaker. Visit him anytime at www.liamodonnell.com or follow him on Twitter @liamodonnell.

MIKE DEAS is an author/illustrator of graphic novels, including *Dalen and Gole* and the *Graphic Guide Adventure* series. While he grew up with a love of illustrative storytelling, Capilano College's Commercial Animation Program helped Mike fine-tune his drawing skills and imagination. Mike and his wife, Nancy, currently live in sunny Victoria, British Columbia. For more information, visit www.deasillustration.com or follow him on Twitter @deasillustration.

Don't miss the first two books in the Tank & Fizz mystery series!

Silver Birch Express Award nominee

Hackmatack Children's Choice Book Award nominee

Tank & Fizz: The Case of the Slime Stampede
9781459808102 • $9.95 • Ages 8-11

The cleaning slimes have escaped, leaving a trail of acidic ooze throughout the schoolyard. Can detective duo Tank & Fizz solve this slimy mystery?

"Young readers will slurp up the gumshoes' gooey first exploit with relish."
—*Kirkus Reviews*

"Something slimy is running amuck in Rockfall Mountain and it isn't the cleaning slimes. This chapter book brims with reader appeal."
—*School Library Journal*